My Life as a Book

JANET TASHJIAN

My Life
as a
Book

with cartoons by
JAKE TASHJIAN

SCHOLASTIC INC.
New York Toronto London Auckland
Sydney Mexico City New Delhi Hong Kong

ISBN 978-0-545-38726-2

Text copyright © 2010 by Janet Tashjian. Illustrations copyright © 2010 by Jake Tashjian. All rights reserved. Published by Scholastic Inc., 557 Broadway, New York, NY 10012, by arrangement with Henry Holt and Company, LLC. SCHOLASTIC and associated logos are trademarks and/or registered trademarks of Scholastic Inc.

12 11 10 9 8 7 6 5 4 3 2 1   11 12 13 14 15 16/0

Printed in the U.S.A.   75

This edition first printing, September 2011

Lexile is a registered trademark of MetaMetrics, Inc.

For Bill Watterson

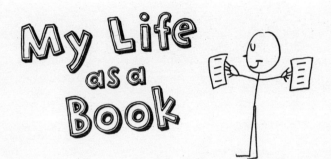

Help!

"I DON'T WANT TO READ THIS BOOK!"

Ever since my teacher said I was a "reluctant reader," I spend every waking minute avoiding my mother and her latest idea of how I should use my time. WASTE my time is more like it.

reluctant

"The librarian said you'd love this book." Mom vaults over a basket of

vaults

laundry, but I'm too fast for her. I dive out my bedroom window onto the roof of the garage. "One chocolate chip per page," she calls.

"That's the old rate. My price has gone up." As soon as my mother starts to climb out after me, I hoist myself through the open attic window. A few minutes later, I hear her at the bottom of the attic stairs.

"Two chocolate chips per page, but that's as high as I'll go, Derek."

While my mother tries to bribe me down from the attic with chocolate, I rummage through the cardboard boxes to see if there's a stick I can use to shoot my way out. Instead, I find a stack of letters my father wrote to my mother when they were dating—yuck—and some old newspapers. When I open one of them up, the headline reads

rummage

LOCAL GIRL FOUND DEAD ON BEACH. The newspaper is from Martha's Vineyard, Massachusetts, and dated ten years ago. (I have to do the math in the dust with my finger.)

I open the attic trapdoor and hang down by my feet. I'm facing my mother upside down, like Peter Parker and Mary Jane in the first Spider-Man movie, except we don't kiss—OBVIOUSLY. I ask Mom about a dead seventeen-year-old girl on an island we've never been to, but she doesn't know what I'm talking about. So I toss down the newspaper. When she picks it up, her expression changes.

obviously

"This has nothing to do with you," she says.

"No kidding," I answer. "I just want to know why we have it."

She yanks me down by the

waistband of my jeans and catches me before I hit the floor.

"Instead of making up a story, you're going to read one." She tucks the newspaper article into her back pocket, then shoves the library book into my hands.

The thing is, I *like* to read. If everyone just left me alone with Calvin, Hobbes, Garfield, Bucky, and Satchel, I could read all day. But forcing a kid to do something as private as reading? My teacher, my mother, and the reading tutor—a nice woman named SATAN!—came up with a new reading system for me this year. They had me keep a list of all the vocabulary words I didn't know. Because I like to draw—my father is a professional illustrator—I took their idea and made it my own.

vocabulary

So instead of writing the vocabulary words, now I *draw* them. Anything to get out of reading.

My parents insist I use this system all the time, so I usually pretend I'm a spy being tortured by Super Evildoers who force me to practice "active reading" or be killed by a foreign assassin. But if everyone thinks I'm spending my summer doing this, they are WRONG, WRONG, WRONG.

assassin

If my life were a book, I'd have my own cool adventures instead of reading about someone else's. If I were the main character in an exciting story rather than some kid who has to sit around and READ all day, I'd spend the summer trying to find out how that girl in the newspaper ended up dead.

adventure

Torture in the Classroom

demented

The next morning Ms. Williams picks up where my mother left off. She passes out the summer reading list, wearing a demented smile and acting as if she's tossing out free candy. I pretend to smash my head on my desk.

Ms. Williams ignores me. "You'll read three books from this list and write a report on one of them.

The way our principal shifted assignments next year, I'm happy to say, I'll be your teacher again in September."

I swear I'm not a troublemaker, but it's like an alien life-form has landed in the classroom wielding assault weapons in each hand. SOMEBODY HAS TO STOP THE MADNESS!

wielding

"Are you saying we have you again next year and we have a report due on the first day of school?" I ask. "That's reading *and* writing homework! For the summer! It's just not doable on my schedule."

My friend Matt thinks this is funny, but I know he'll enjoy the show from the sidelines without backing me up.

The teacher's voice has that same weary tone as my mother's. "Please

weary

tell us about all these summer activities—I can't wait to hear."

"That's the whole thing," I say. "You can't plan when you're going to pelt the UPS truck with water balloons or when you'll dig up worms and put them in Mr. Parker's mail slot or when you'll dip your action figures in paint and flick them at your friend with a lacrosse stick until you're both covered in painty stripes. Summer's like a pajama-and-cereal day—if you try to plan it out ahead of time, you wreck it."

Matt waves his fist in the air as if he's the one giving Ms. Williams a hard time. The teacher places the reading list squarely in front of me. "I'm afraid you'll have to try and fit in three of these books during all that fun."

pelt

I like Ms. Williams, but I wouldn't complain if she was kidnapped by crazed bank robbers in need of a getaway car.

kidnapped

The reading list—unfortunately—isn't going anywhere either. I stare at it and wonder what I've gotten myself into. One of the books is about a kid and his dog over summer vacation and all the exciting things they do together and the lessons the boy learns.

I have a dog and—trust me—that stuff only happens in books.

Playing James Bond

Matt and I are at the mall looking at DVDs and comic books. His mother is trying on shoes a few stores down, but we imagine she isn't with us and that we came here on our own.

My favorite clerk, Jamie, wraps DVDs in plastic then seals them with a blow-dryer. When his boss isn't looking, Jamie pretends to stick his finger in the electrical outlet while

electrical

he aims the blow-dryer at his head so his hair flies around like he's been shocked. I laugh more than Matt does, but that's because Jamie is Matt's older brother and he never thinks anything Jamie does is funny.

shocked

As we scan the new action comedies, I tell Matt about the newspaper article I found in the attic. "I want to find out more about the girl who drowned," I say. "Do you think Jamie can help?"

"He's more interested in girls that are alive." Matt points to Jamie blowing the hair of two high school girls giggling by the cash register. Jamie's boss coughs with disapproval and says he's going down the hall for a coffee. That's all Matt and I need to hear.

disapproval

"Come on, Jamie. Your boss won't

impress

be back for at least ten minutes," I say.

Matt starts to hum the James Bond theme song. Jamie tries to impress the girls by being a good brother, so he presses the button that lowers the store's gate. The metal bars come down slowly from the ceiling while Matt and I run through the store as if we're spies being chased by bad guys. Then, when the gate's just a few feet from the ground, we roll under it and escape at the last second.

Jamie waves to us from the other side of the bars and tells us we look like monkeys at the zoo.

"Very funny," Matt says. "Raise the gate so we can do it again."

Instead, Jamie takes packing peanuts from the box of DVDs and starts throwing them as if we're monkeys and it's feeding time.

"Don't be a knucklehead," I say. "Let's do it again before your boss comes back."

knucklehead

But Jamie is focused on the girls and has blocked us out completely.

"Just where you two belong— behind bars."

I turn around and see Carly Rodriquez, the smartest girl in our class. I tell her we're in the middle of re-enacting a James Bond movie, and if she doesn't get out of the way, we can't be responsible for her safety.

She waves a green plastic bag in our faces like she's got the secret code we spies are searching for. "I just picked out my summer reading books. I got two extra ones in case I finish the others early."

envious

Teacher's pet, as usual. I tell Jamie his boss is coming back with the coffee, and he immediately hits the button to raise the gate. When it's a foot off the floor, Matt and I roll back into the store. Carly almost looks a little envious of our game.

Jamie peeks down the hall. "You liar, he's not coming."

"I know." I take a handful of change from the HAVE A PENNY, LEAVE A PENNY tray on the counter, then run down to meet Matt in the poster section. I see Carly at the other end of the store, smiling as she pages through one of her new books. This time I'm the one who's envious.

Why Call Her a Babysitter If I'm Not a Baby?

When my parents leave for their Thursday-night date, I offer my babysitter, Amy, a truce. Usually I torture her by locking myself in the bathroom, running the water, and overflowing the bathtub, or taking my old bike from the basement and riding it down the front hall stairs. Last time I did, I skidded into my father's worktable and his markers ended up all over the house.

truce

skidded

"I'll make a deal with you," I say. "If you help me do some research, I'll go to bed on time with no fuss. I swear."

She stops texting her friends and looks at me suspiciously. "Is this for a school project?"

"Kind of." Since my mother grabbed the newspaper article away from me the other day, I searched every wastebasket in the house with no luck. All I can remember about the news story is the date.

When Amy goes back to texting, I stick my face between her and the phone and ask if she can find more information on the computer. She jumps at the chance to use my father's superfast laptop and types in MARTHA'S VINEYARD DROWNING, as well as the year. Several articles pop up, but I finally spot the short piece

I found in the attic. The girl's name is Susan James. I ask Amy if there's anything else.

"Why are you asking *me*?"

I tell Amy I've cornered Mom twice, but she gets angrier each time I ask. I even heard her talking to Dad about it in the den with the door shut.

"'You can always write to the newspaper if you're that desperate to know."

desperate

"But then I'd have to WRITE." I decide I don't like Amy's attitude, so I break our truce, grab my dog, Bodi, and lock us in my mother's car. After a few minutes of trying to coax me out, Amy gives up and goes inside.

coax

I scrunch down in the backseat and think about a girl Amy's age who died. I bury my head into Bodi's chocolate fur and wonder what that must've been like for her parents, her brothers and sisters, if she had any, or even her dog. As if he knows what I'm thinking, Bodi moves in closer and puts his head on my leg. I imagine waves crashing on an island I've never been to but then am startled by bright lights behind me. Mom and Dad, home early.

startled

When I jump out of the car, Bodi does too. "We were just cleaning it. What a mess!"

Amy meets us in the driveway and holds out her hand to get paid. "He locked them in again. Plus, he was obsessed with an article about some girl who drowned. Mrs. Fallon, I tried my best, I really did."

obsessed

My mother gives her a twenty, and Amy is back on her cell before my father can offer to walk her home. I yell across the street for

Bodi to stop eating the food Mr. Jennings leaves out for his cat.

My mother holds open the back door. "I have no idea why I saved that article," she says. "I must've been interested in something on the back."

"There was an ad for a furniture store."

"See? I was probably looking at couches."

"On Martha's Vineyard?"

Mom tries hard not to get annoyed. "I know you have a curious mind, but maybe you can focus on something else. Tomorrow's the last day of school—let's have a great summer, okay?" She shoots me that smile she wears when she'd give everything she owns to get me to behave for more than just a few minutes.

annoyed

I tell her we won't be doing anything in school tomorrow besides watching a DVD so it's fine if I stay home. But she's not buying it and sends me up to brush my teeth.

Later (I didn't brush my teeth) I trace the letters S–U–S–A–N J–A–M–E–S on the wall. Bodi looks up from his spot at the foot of my bed and watches as if he can read. Maybe if he could, the summer reading list wouldn't be such a chore. I tell myself to stop thinking about bad stuff; after all, tomorrow is the start of vacation, the start of sleeping late, the end of being prodded every day by teachers with their mental Tasers to LEARN, LEARN, LEARN.

investigate

Tomorrow is also the day I start to investigate what my mother is trying to hide.

Finally!

The last day of school should be the best day of the year, but it's a disaster. Ms. Williams can't get the DVD player to work, so she points to everything in the room and makes us spell it like we're back in kindergarten. When she points to a photo of Mr. Demetri, I spell T-H-E W-O-R-S-T P-R-I-N-C-I-P-A-L W-E H-A-V-E E-V-E-R H-A-D instead.

punishment

appreciates

fantasy

I thought I did a great job with all that spelling, but Ms. Williams is not amused and makes me write out the multiplication tables for punishment. No one appreciates a good joke anymore, that's the problem.

When I get to my locker, Joe Brennan is waiting for me. Joe used to be one of the smallest kids in our school, but he had a growth spurt last fall and now he's the biggest. Joe isn't smart enough to use his new size to shake down kids for lunch money. Instead, his favorite trick is getting in your face with his junk-food breath and making you listen to his lame made-up stories. Trust me, losing your cash is a hundred times better than his fantasy tales about talking gerbils and magic turtles.

I lean against my locker to escape

his foul breath. From the orange crumbs nesting between his teeth, I assume he's been eating Cheetos.

"Hey, Derek," he says, "are you around this summer? I'm working on a great story about a cat with wings who's afraid of heights."

"Sounds interesting." I tell him another lie—that I'll be in skateboard camp in Venice Beach and won't be around.

He doesn't buy it. "You'll be hanging around the neighborhood with that stupid old mutt retriever of yours, same as every summer."

"My dog might be old and a mutt, but he's not stupid." I can feel the handle of the locker pressing into my back as I lean away from the orange-y crumbs shooting out of Joe's mouth.

When I burp in his face, Joe finally lets go of my T-shirt. I hurry back to the classroom and run smack into Ms. Williams.

She places a book in my hand. "Consider this an end-of-school present."

It's one of the books from our reading list.

"Since it's not a library or classroom book," she continues, "you can write in it. I made you some notes in the margins. I hope you find them helpful."

"You're giving me a used book?"

She ignores me. "And don't forget to keep drawing your vocabulary words."

Ms. Williams obviously doesn't realize I'm trying to escape because she continues to block the door. We move side to side in the doorway like two old people dancing. As if on cue, Carly appears beside me. She smiles sweetly to Ms. Williams, then shoots me the evil eye to stop blocking the entrance to her precious classroom.

precious

I move out of the way and thank Ms. Williams for the book. When Carly realizes the teacher gave me a present and not her, she lets out a pathetic noise that sounds as if she's been punched in the gut.

"Carly, are you ready to take Ginger home?" Ms. Williams asks.

Carly volunteered—of course—to watch the class hedgehog for the summer. She stands near Ginger's crate like a Secret Service agent guarding the president. Maybe she'll fall asleep with Ginger on her lap this summer and wake up with marks on her legs from Ginger's quills.

When the bell rings at the end

quills

of the day, most of the girls hug each other good-bye at the lockers, milking every last second of school time until next September. I vault over the hedge near the school entrance and skid to a halt in front of the crossing guard. When she tells me to have a nice summer, I shout back that I intend to. At home, I throw my backpack onto the porch and let out Bodi. I think about grabbing his leash but decide against it. We're finally free!

Making Fruit Grenades

Matt and I get my markers and draw grids on the avocados piled on the kitchen counter. When we finish, we take them outside and stack them like cannonballs. Then we "borrow" three bags of potting soil from the garage, empty them into the middle of the driveway, and build two large mounds. We take our places behind the opposite hills.

grid

"If we were still in school, we'd be in Social Studies right now." He pelts me with one of the avocados, which lands in green chunks on my sneaker.

I hurl an avocado back but miss. "Even worse than Social Studies, we'd be in assembly watching Mr. Demetri sing stupid folk songs and play his guitar."

explosion

I'm not sure if it's our explosion noises that bring my mother out of the house, but when I look up she's standing on the porch watching us bomb each other.

"They are hand grenades," I inform her.

"I got it." She looks at me with that face that tells me I've messed up once again. "I was going to use those avocados for dinner."

I point to the green mush all over the driveway and our clothes. "They're still edible. Why don't you bring out a bag of chips?"

She closes the door without answering and I know we won't be seeing chips anytime soon. Besides, Bodi has already eaten the biggest chunks of avocado off the driveway.

The next person to appear on the porch is my father. One of the good things about having a father who works from home is that he's always around. Unfortunately, that's one of the bad things too.

He places a box of large garbage bags on the stairs. "I assume you two are planning on putting all that potting soil back, right?"

"Right," Matt and I both pretend to agree.

edible

Dad takes a ten-dollar bill out of his wallet and places it under the box. "Then you can walk to the store and replace those avocados."

My father keeps talking, but Matt and I are only focused on the crisp ten-dollar bill calling our names. I'm thinking seven, maybe eight, king-sized candy bars; I bet Matt is thinking the same thing. When my father finally goes inside, Matt and I dive for the money. He gets to it before I do.

"Giant bag of popcorn, a tub of ice cream, or a box of cupcakes with sprinkles?" He snaps the bill at me like it's a towel in gym class.

Matt and I skateboard to the grocery store, and I ask the man in the produce department if there are any avocados on sale. He brings out several from the back room that are

produce

much cheaper than the ones in the bins. Matt and I have enough money left over to get a quart of chocolate fudge ice cream. We take utensils and napkins from the salad bar, then sit on our skateboards out back to eat.

utensils

"Guess where my mom decided we're going on vacation this summer?" Matt asks.

I shrug and dig at the vein of fudge buried along the side of the carton.

"Martha's Vineyard. Isn't that where the girl in that newspaper article drowned?"

I suddenly feel envious of Matt's vacation plans. Not because his family is going away and we're not, but because he is one step closer to having a real adventure than I am.

"Why don't you ask your mom if

you can take me? I took you to San Francisco last year, remember?" Since I'm an only child, my parents often let me take friends on vacation. Sometimes I take Matt, and sometimes I just take Bodi.

Matt tries to get at the fudge by fencing his spoon with mine. I finally move my spoon out of the way to make room for his.

fencing

"I'll ask my mom if you can come. But it's three thousand miles to the Vineyard. I'm not sure what she's going to say."

I whisper a prayer from inside my head straight to Matt's mom. *Say yes; I'll be good. Say yes; I'll be good.*

When we finally get home, my mother tests the avocados in her hand and tells me they're overripe and will be brown inside. She sweeps

them off the counter into the
trash, then wipes off my chocolate
mustache with the dish towel. She
uses a little too much force, but I
don't complain. We have takeout
Chinese food for dinner and I don't
complain about that either. I take a
thumbtack and fasten the slip from
my fortune cookie onto the bulletin
board in my room: A STORY WILL
UNFOLD BEFORE YOU. I bury myself
underneath the covers and hope it
will be true. If only I could get the
guys at the fortune cookie factory
to do my summer book report too.

I focus on my new plan—to
talk Matt's mom into letting me
accompany them on vacation.

mustache

accompany

Poor Dad

Even though it's summer vacation, I don't mind going to work with my dad. He's an artist who draws storyboards for films, and today he's working with a director shooting a horror movie. It's great to spend the day on a movie set scattered with fake body parts and chainsaws. While my father meets with the director about how he wants the storyboard

scattered

to look, I bug the prop man to give me his recipe for fake blood. The guy laughs but won't let me in on his secret.

When Dad and I eat lunch in the studio cafeteria, I check out his sketches. They're the kind of basic drawings I make for my vocabulary words but with better backgrounds and from different angles.

I laugh when I see an actress with pretend blood on her arms, eating a salad at the next table. But Dad doesn't pay attention to her; he's looking at the man she's with, a young guy with cool glasses and a goatee. Dad looks down at his drawings and suddenly seems sad. I ask him what's the matter.

goatee

"They get younger and younger all the time," he says.

animation

"The actors?"

He shakes his head. "The artists. They come out of school now with all this animation experience. It's tough to compete." He tucks his sketches under his jacket on the chair beside him.

I know the conversation is going to come back around to me. When you're an only child, it always does.

"That's why it's important for you to keep up with your schoolwork. It's a tough job market out there."

I want to remind him that I'm only twelve, but he seems depressed, so I don't bother. When we head back home, I don't ask him to stop at the comic book store in case that will make him feel even worse.

Later, when Dad falls asleep on the couch watching the news, I get an idea. I take one of the markers from his worktable and start to make him a little younger looking. My father sleeps as heavily as a giant woolly mammoth and doesn't wake up until my mother walks into the room and screams.

"Derek! What are you doing?"

"Just practicing my artistic skills."

She starts to laugh when she sees my father's face, but then her eyes widen. I follow her gaze to my hand and realize I am holding a permanent marker. My father rises and catches his reflection in the living room mirror.

permanent

reflection

"Derek Martin Jeremy Fallon, you have gone too far!" Mom says.

"I thought I'd help Dad keep up with the young guys, that's all."

My father looks at the long, wide

encourage

sideburns and half a mustache. "It's actually not that bad."

"Jeremy!" my mother yells. "Don't encourage him!" She runs into the kitchen and comes back with a dish towel, but my father's new facial hair isn't going anywhere soon.

dentures

She rubs his mouth with so much force, I wonder if he's going to need dentures when she's through with him. As I march up to my room, I make a mental list of all the cool stuff I could do with a set of fake teeth.

The next morning when my father comes downstairs, I try to hide my laughter. He's still got some of the sideburns I drew on him and he's wearing a black T-shirt that's too small. He combed his hair with my mother's gel, so it's sticking up in a million directions. As funny as my dad looks, his attempt at being cool makes me sad. Now it's my turn to give advice.

"You shouldn't worry about all those young guys getting all the jobs," I say. "You're a good illustrator. You just have to do what you told me—keep at it."

He looks at me like I'm actually saying something that makes sense instead of just regurgitating the same old stuff he always tells me.

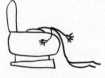

regurgitating

"You're exactly right. We'll both dedicate ourselves to our studies this summer."

And just like that, I realize that by trying to help my dad I've committed myself to even more work. You know that saying, "Nice guys finish last"? It's 100 percent true.

Forcing My Parents
to Admit the Truth

bouquet

I pick a bouquet of coneflowers from Mr. Parker's garden for Matt's mom to persuade her to let me go on vacation with them. I also help Matt sweep his sidewalk and water their container garden. I even help carry his mother's six bags of groceries into the house. But when Matt finally gets an answer, his mom says no.

Matt and I plug his sister's old sunlamp into the outlet on the side of the house to try to set the grass on fire.

"Is it because Massachusetts is so far away?" I ask.

"No. I think she decided against it after talking to your mom."

"My mother told her I couldn't go?"

"I think so. Sorry, dude. I tried."

Matt's sister Tanya comes running out of the house and asks if we're insane—she says that it's drought season and we could start a fire that might burn for days. In the middle of her speech, I tell Matt I have to leave. Ever since Tanya started babysitting around the neighborhood, she's been impossible. Bodi runs alongside me when I skateboard home.

As I slalom between the traffic

drought

interrogate

cones I set up in the street, I imagine a giant-size sunlamp I could use to interrogate my mother. Since I don't have one, I climb onto the roof of the garage with the croquet set instead. It takes a few swings before I nail the satellite dish with the green ball. Moments later, my father storms outside.

"If I miss a hole-in-one in this tournament because you're messing around with the satellite dish, I swear to God, I'll use that mallet on you! Put the dish back where it was and get down here this minute!"

improved

"I'm not coming down till I find out why you won't let me go to Martha's Vineyard." I take another shot and hit the satellite dish again. My skill has definitely improved since I started doing this in third grade.

My father screams for my mother, who comes outside with two pairs of reading glasses tucked into her hair like a headband, another on the neckline of her shirt, and a fourth pair actually on her eyes. Usually she can never find them, but now it seems every pair in the house has found her.

"Derek, not again. Please!"

I tell her I'm not coming down until she tells me why I can't go on vacation with Matt. My father throws up his hands in surrender and goes inside.

surrender

"I didn't want you going on vacation with Matt's family because the Vineyard is all the way across the country. It's too far."

"You didn't want me going because you're afraid I'll find out about that girl who drowned." I correct myself. "You're afraid I'll find out about Susan James."

It's as if the sound of Susan's name loosens something inside my mother. Even from my perch on the roof, I can see she's suddenly sad.

"Get off the roof and I'll tell you everything." Her tone is so calm that I toss down the balls and mallets. But as soon as I hit the ground, she yanks me into the house and serves up a big slice of MomMad. "I don't want you up there again, do you hear me? It's not safe, and that satellite dish is expensive."

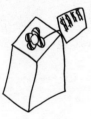

expensive

I squirm away from her and sit at the kitchen table. She sighs and sits down beside me.

"We rented a house for a week in Martha's Vineyard one August on our way back from visiting Grandma in Boston. You were two years old."

I sit on my hands so I won't fidget while she's talking.

fidget

"Some people from the studio where Dad was working were also on vacation there and invited us for an early dinner. We didn't know anyone on the island, so we called a babysitting service. They sent over this nice college student with excellent references to sit for a few hours."

"Susan James?"

My mother's voice gets even more quiet. "Yes. She was a freshman at the University of Maine living at home with her parents on the Vineyard for the summer."

I try to sit quietly, even though it's incredibly difficult not to interrupt with a million questions.

"We told her to stay at the house, but as soon as we left, she strapped you in the car and took you to South Beach. By the time the woman from the service called us, you were back at the house asleep, safe and sound. We couldn't believe it when the woman told us Susan had drowned."

I still want more details. "But how?"

My mother seems to weigh how much to tell me before she speaks. "I  guess you wandered into the water, and Susan went in to get you. She pushed you to shore but the riptide pulled her back in. I didn't tell you because I didn't want you to think it was your fault."

riptide

Why couldn't I have left that stupid newspaper article alone?

If I had known the drowning had anyway to do with me, I never would've asked all those questions. I should've known extra reading would be hazardous to my health.

hazardous

My mother leaves the kitchen and comes back with a folder. "Susan's mother and I wrote several letters over the years."

I look through the folder and find a Christmas card with a snowman on skis.

"I know it wasn't our fault or yours—Susan never should've left the house with you—but I felt guilty anyway." Mom puts her hand on mine while I'm still holding the card. "I can't imagine what it's like to lose a child."

I suddenly realize it's Thursday, my parents' date night. "Should you cancel Amy?" I ask. "She's not my favorite babysitter, but I don't want to accidentally kill her too."

Mom takes the card away. "You were not responsible. You were two years old—you didn't do anything wrong." When she dials Amy's number to tell her she and my father decided not to go out tonight, I know it's not because she's afraid for Amy's life but because Mom doesn't want to let me out of her sight. I can't blame her; I don't feel like straying too far from home either. She asks Dad to pick up some takeout from the Greek restaurant near the pier.

straying

The three of us sit in the backyard and watch Bodi run back and forth along the fence, chasing the terrier next door. As I eat my lamb kebab, I finally get why my mother didn't tell me about Susan. I spent a week bugging her for details; now that I have them, I'm more miserable than before. It seems my curious mind got the better of me, that this time I should've left things alone. I poke the wooden skewer into the palm of my hand until my father tells me to stop.

skewer

Trying to Forget

For the next few days, I try to forget about the newspaper article, but I can't. Even though I know the truth about what happened, I can't stop nagging Mom with a thousand questions. What did Susan James look like? Where did we stay on the Vineyard? Eventually, my mother puts a halt to my interrogation and tells me the subject is now closed.

eventually

A few years ago when the commercial building next door went up for sale, my parents bought it, and my Mom moved her practice there. She's been a veterinarian for more than twelve years. She also has a boarding business she calls "Pet Camp" and a grooming service she calls "Pet Spa," which makes me think of dogs getting massages and lying around with cucumbers on their eyes. In reality, it's more like picking off ticks and getting the gunk out of their ears.

veterinarian

I'm so glad to be on vacation, I help Mom tack new photos onto the huge collage in her waiting room. When people first bring their animals to her, she always takes a picture of them with their dogs, cats, lizards, ferrets, hamsters, or birds, then

collage

despise

elderly

places them in her collage that now takes up almost the entire wall.

"I saw Maria Rodriquez at the store the other day," she says.

"Who?"

"Carly's mom. We talked about you two getting together this summer."

"First of all, I'm too old for you to be setting up playdates. Second of all, she's a brownnosing Goody Two-shoes, who I despise."

"Oh, come on—she can't be that bad." Mom tacks a photo of an elderly man with a cockatoo on his shoulder to the wall.

"Trust me, she *is*."

When she's finished, my mother takes a novel from her purse, kicks off her shoes, and settles into one of the comfy waiting-room chairs. I don't buy it.

"If you're doing this as an example of how much fun reading is, it's not working."

She closes the book but keeps her finger in the page. "Believe it or not, Derek, not everything has to do with you. I have a free hour and just want to relax—do you mind?" She waves me off and goes back to her book.

I leave her in the waiting room and visit the animals in the kennel: a basset hound named Lionel who's here while his owners are on vacation and two gray cats I've never seen before. I give Lionel a treat from the canister on the counter, then sneak a peek at my mom, who's still reading even though she doesn't know I'm watching. She has on the same content face that Carly had at Jamie's store, and I wonder if

canister

content

books make only girls happy. Then I remember my dad and Uncle Bob both like to read, and I start to wonder what's wrong with *me*. Maybe it's like blue eyes and blond hair—there's a reading gene some people get or don't get at birth.

When my mother turns the page, she spots me near the door. "It's the perfect time to start one of those books on your list."

"No thanks."

"I'll get us some cookies."

"No thanks."

"I'll help you with the words you don't know."

"No thanks."

"Two chocolate chips per page?" She pats the seat next to her, an invitation for me to sit down. "Let me see the illustrations you did of your vocabulary words so far."

invitation

I run back to the house and get my sketchbook, sit down next to her, and show her my drawings.

She smiles. "Some of these remind me of your father's. Did you know he used to get yelled at when he was young for drawing all over his homework?"

I shake my head.

"One of his teachers called his drawings 'messy doodles' and 'a waste of time.' I bet she'd be surprised to find out he gets paid to do them now."

This gives me an idea, and I draw a picture of Dad as a kid using a giant pencil as a battering ram, knocking down the school's exit door. I choose the colors carefully, the way I always do. When I finish, Mom asks if she can have it. I say yes and she tacks it to the wall next to the main desk.

I spend the rest of the afternoon checking the details of my illustrations. I may not make my bed, pick up my clothes, put away my DVDs, or wipe the puddles of water off the floor after I take a bath, but I'm never messy with my drawings.

A New Friend

One of Mom's assistant vets is on vacation, so she lets me come to work with her again. Usually, she has a few cats and dogs in the boarding cages, but this time when I go into the back room, I'm surprised to find a monkey.

assistant

"His name is Pedro. He's a capuchin who's been trained to work with people in wheelchairs. Pedro lives with a good friend of mine who just moved to Venice Beach."

"He's wearing a diaper!"

"So he doesn't make a mess."

"What does he do around the house?"

"All kinds of things. Capuchins start training when they're young. They make very nice companions."

companion

Suddenly a boring day of tagging along with my mother becomes a day full of possibility and adventure.

But Mom's spoil-his-fun antennae

antennae

pop up. "Even though Pedro is trained, monkeys can still bite. I don't want you getting any ideas." She explains that she usually doesn't treat monkeys, but because she had a lot of training with exotic pets in vet school, she's able to help out her friend. Then she steers me away from the capuchin and asks me to trim the cocker spaniel's nails. I've been doing this for a while, so I know how to fasten the dog's leash to the table and get him in position so he doesn't move around. I even know how far down to trim so I don't cut inside the nail where it could hurt.

But as I'm grooming the spaniel, all I can think about is Pedro. In my imagination, my mother goes out to lunch and I let the monkey out of his cage, call Matt, and we watch action movies while Pedro does our chores. When he's finished, he sits between us on the couch and goes crazy during the explosion scenes. We even skateboard down the street with Pedro alternating between our two boards. In reality, my morning is much less exciting. I cut the dog's toenails while Pedro scratches himself.

alternating

After sweeping up hair and

putting away the heartworm pills, I decide Pedro and I both need some fresh air. While my mother is in one of the rooms tending to a cat that swallowed her owner's bracelet, I undo the latch on Pedro's cage and slip him onto my shoulder. He's surprisingly light and sits quietly on my head while I sneak out the back to our house next door. My father's car is gone, so Pedro and I have the place to ourselves.

I break up a candy bar into a bowl to test Pedro's microwave skills so we can dip strawberries into the melted chocolate. Instead, he eats the chocolate without even trying to use the microwave. I wonder if the woman in Venice Beach lied to my mother when she said Pedro helps around the house.

I decide what Pedro needs is fun, not work, so I find my old cowboy outfit in the basement. I poke another hole in the holster strap, then fasten it around Pedro's waist. He takes the cowboy hat off the counter and puts it on as if he's just been *waiting* for this. He must watch a lot of Westerns with his owner because Pedro takes the toy guns from the holsters and wields them like he's tearing up an old saloon. Bodi wanders in from the doggie door, then barks like a lunatic when he sees Pedro.

lunatic

"Calm down," I say. "You two are going to be great friends." I pick up Pedro and place him on Bodi as if he's a horse. Either he wants Pedro off his back or he's willing to play along, because Bodi takes off through the

shrieking

house with Pedro holding on to his collar for dear life. Bodi is barking and Pedro's shrieking, so I start screaming too and grab the gun that Pedro dropped. The three of us race through the house when I suddenly see my mother standing in the doorway. The expression on her face is scarier than an actress in one of Dad's horror movies.

When Mom grabs Bodi by the collar, Pedro climbs up her arm and sits on her shoulder. She hands Bodi a treat from the pocket of her lab coat, then turns to me.

"I'm signing you up for summer camp."

"NO! We decided I would stay home and play this summer!"

She points around the living room to the tipped chair and my dad's portfolio all over the floor. "If kidnapping a monkey and running wild through the house is your idea of 'play,' we need to redefine the term."

portfolio

I still would rather be home, but I suppose there are worse things than doing sports all summer. I tell her I'll look through some camp Web sites and find a good one tonight.

She shakes her head.

"Skateboard camp?" I ask.

"Not this time."

"Rock climbing camp?"

"No."

"Karate camp?"

"No again."

I suddenly fear for my life.

"You have too much time on your hands," she says. "You're going to Learning Camp."

accomplish

"NO!"

"Yes. There are six weeks left of vacation—think of all the things you can accomplish. You'll start school in September ahead of the game."

"But what about lying on the grass and staring at clouds and playing kickball and making forts and watching *The Three Stooges* and eating Popsicles and—"

"Enough! You're not five years old anymore. You need to start getting serious."

"I'm twelve! Plus, it's summer—*no one's* supposed to be serious!"

It almost seems like Pedro knows what's going on because he wags his finger as if he disapproves of my behavior.

"I was going to shave him with Dad's electric razor," I say. "But I didn't! I used good judgment. I don't need to go to Learning Camp!" I don't tell her that the only reason I didn't shave Pedro was because I couldn't find Dad's razor.

judgment

Bodi sticks his head between my legs, a move he always makes when he knows I need comfort. My mother brings Pedro back to her office and tells me we'll sign up for Learning Camp after dinner.

Why can't grown-ups just let a kid play with a dog and a monkey in peace?

I Try Not to
Kill the Babysitter

impulse

discipline

The next day my mother hires Amy to "keep me company," which is really just another way to say "babysit." I overheard my parents talking in their room last night when I was supposed to be asleep. You don't need to be a brain surgeon to string the words *impulse control* and *discipline* into a story no kid wants to read. When they're done, my father tapes Ms. Williams's summer reading list onto the refrigerator. They tell me Learning Camp is all set, but *I* tell *them* the best place for me to spend the rest of the summer is leaning against the large palm tree in our backyard with a stack of comic books and Bodi. It's a discussion I don't have a chance of winning. I feel like I'm trapped in *Prison in July*, a horror movie I just made up.

When Amy first started baby-sitting, she used to make my lunches; now she twirls her hair and points to the cupboard for me to make my own peanut butter and banana sandwich. I can, of course. I just preferred it when I looked for funny videos online and she made lunch. I cut the sandwich on the diagonal

preferred

and put the pieces on a plate to prove I don't need her help to make a nice meal.

"I killed one of my first baby-sitters," I say. "So I wouldn't try anything if I were you."

"I'm really scared," she says, then tears off a corner of my sandwich without asking.

lethal

"Seriously. Babysitting for me can be lethal. I feel I should warn you."

"For ten dollars an hour, I'll take my chances," Amy says.

I think about offering her twelve dollars an hour to go home, but I'm pretty cheap when it comes to spending my own money on boring stuff like babysitters.

"Your mom told me about that girl who drowned. Don't expect that kind of service from me."

For once I can't think of a snappy comeback, choosing instead to concentrate on my lunch.

concentrate

Amy leans back in her chair. "I don't know anyone who died. My second-grade teacher's husband got killed in a car accident, but I never met him."

accident

"I didn't really know Susan either," I say. I don't tell her that last night in bed, I imagined that I drowned with Susan. The thought kept me awake until Bodi made his dreaming noises and stopped me from doing any more thinking.

I give Amy the rest of my sandwich and start making another. Just then, Matt bursts into the kitchen.

"They're delivering bricks for our new patio," he says. "There's a huge eighteen-wheeler in the driveway. Let's take my old action figures and put them in front of the tires so when the guy drives away, he'll squash them like grapes."

Matt doesn't have to ask twice. I tell Amy I'll be at Matt's, but she barely hears me because she's back on her phone.

As Matt and I line up his old toys in front of the giant tires, I find a small plastic raccoon. I used to have this same action figure, a present in some meal package from a fast-food restaurant. Although he's made of plastic, his kind eyes remind me of Bodi's, and I don't have the heart to squish him. I put the raccoon back in Matt's toy bin and take out some happy elves instead.

Matt and I are ecstatic when the

ecstatic

driver pulls away; he even blasts his horn several times. But the toys are not as flattened as we'd hoped, so we head to the garage to see what else we can use. We find a bag of stones and Tanya's old rock polisher that looks like a cement mixer. We lock the elves inside, then make noises like they're screaming to get out.

flattened

Surprisingly, it's not as much fun as I thought. I realize Matt is having a blast, and *I'm* the problem. Learning Camp starts Monday, and it weighs on me. Suppose I'm the worst student there? I have to work so hard to keep up during the school year—do I have to fake my way through all summer too? The thought of one more person cracking the whip about LEARNING makes me want to jump into the cement mixer with these crazy elves.

I tell Matt I have to go and spend the rest of the afternoon lying in my backyard staring up at the clouds, Bodi by my side.

My Father
Tries to Help

Dad sits me down at the kitchen table to organize the next day.

"I'll drop you at camp at nine," he says.

"NINE? That means I have to get up in the eights."

"Actually, you have to get up in the sevens. It's half an hour away."

Learning Camp is one thing, but an hour a day in the car with one

organize

successful

convinced

of my parents trying to tell me how hard I have to work to be successful is another thing altogether. I realize I have to quickly locate my MP3 player and headphones.

Bodi barely opens his eyes when I toss him the bone from last night's dinner, so I yell upstairs and ask my mother to take a look at him.

She comes down wearing her headset and holding her cell. I'm not sure if it's because she's a doctor, but she's convinced cell phones can give you brain cancer, so she always uses a headset.

Mom hangs up with her friend and looks into Bodi's eyes. She feels his throat, then his belly.

"Is he okay?" I ask twice before she answers.

"Bodi's thirteen now. That's old for a dog."

I pray she doesn't use this as an example of how math comes in handy in real life, but my father beats her to the punch. I hate how parents think they have to use everything that happens as some kind of lesson.

"Seven dog years equals one human year, right? So seven times thirteen equals . . ."

He waits for my answer like an FBI agent interrogating a spy. Thankfully, my mother saves me the embarrassment of not knowing the answer.

embarrassment

"Actually, seven to one is the old rule," Mom says. "Weight and breed are factors too. It's more like he's eighty."

I'm grateful to be off the hook, but then she spoils the moment.

grateful

"See how important math is?"

They both look at me with such desperate smiles, I want to smash my head into the tile counter.

"I just care about Bodi," I say. "Not about stupid math."

My mom thinks he's okay but she'll give him a full workup in the morning.

"I obviously can't go to camp," I say. "I need to be here while you run tests."

"Believe it or not, I know what I'm doing," she says. "Bodi will be fine until you get home."

variations

I try variations on this plan with no success. But maybe Bodi just needed a rest because when it's time for me to go to bed, he follows me upstairs with no problem.

The next morning when I wake up, my mother is sitting on the bed, petting Bodi.

"Is he okay? Because I can definitely stay home from camp."

"He's fine," she says. She reaches into the pocket of her robe and hands me a banana and a protein bar.

protests

I ignore my mother's protests and feed half of the banana to Bodi.

As soon as he gets in the car, my father takes my headphones.

"We've got some quality time ahead of us," he says. "I thought we could discuss one of the books you're reading."

I try to guess our speed so I can figure out the best time to hurl myself out of the car. I imagine myself tumbling along the side of the road, then eating berries and roots in the woods for the rest of the summer.

"Derek? What do you say?"

I bang my head repeatedly against

repeatedly

the side window. When Dad tells me to stop, I open the window, stick my head out, then press the button so the glass squishes my head on its way back up.

"Derek!"

By the time I let down the window, he's turned on the radio. He's shaking his head, probably thinking about how he's failing as a father. I'm just glad I can sit here on my way to Summer Prison in peace.

Isn't This Fun?

After we register, the camp leaders divide us into groups. Mine is called the Mustangs. The leaders show us where to store our possessions and give us directions to the outdoor work areas. I figure things can't get any worse until I see a girl filling out her name tag at the registration table. Just as I'm about to make a run for it, she spots me.

register

possessions

"What are *you* doing here?" Carly asks.

"I was about to ask you the same question."

She shrugs. "My mother works, so I go to different camps every summer."

I know it's only a matter of time before she interrogates me, so I beat her to the punch. "Don't ask about the summer reading list because I haven't even started."

"I wasn't going to ask you anything." She leaves me by the table and approaches the camp leader. She's probably going to try and be that teacher's pet too.

For a brief moment on the drive in, I thought *maybe* I'll be one of the smartest kids here, *maybe* I won't be the one who needs extra help.

I'm sick of feeling like an old broken-down horse on a racetrack that everybody has to encourage from the sidelines. I hoped Learning Camp could be different. Seeing Carly guarantees it won't be.

Our leader's name is Margot, and she reminds me of the actress I saw on the horror set last week. Imagining her with blood gushing from her nostrils and ears makes the first session go by much faster.

enthusiasm

"First item on the schedule—geography!" Margot has so much enthusiasm that I wonder if she'll pop an artery for real.

She gives us maps and asks us to plan trips to various cities around the country. Here's where *I* want to travel to: ANYWHERE BUT HERE.

artery

An hour later, Margot hands

out Popsicles and tells us to take a break. I check to see if everyone got a Popsicle before I pretend I didn't and take another. I pull my markers and pad from my pack for a minute of peace.

No such luck.

"Can I see?"

I look up to find Margot eating potato chips and pointing to my sketchbook. I shrug and show her my drawings.

"That's how you do your vocabulary words? Cool."

I get back to my illustration.

"Does your school have summer reading? God, I used to *despise* those lists." She holds out the potato chip bag, and I take a handful.

criminal

"Imagine telling people what to read," she continues. "It's criminal!"

"Exactly!" I agree.

"When I was your age, all I wanted to read was Garfield."

"I love him, but for me, it's Calvin and Hobbes."

She nods, as if remembering her own favorite comic strip. "Books aren't as fun without the pictures."

"I know exactly what you mean." I want Margot to move in with us and talk some sense into my parents.

Margot tosses the chips bag in the trash and wipes her hands on her denim shorts. "You want to know a secret?"

furiously

I nod furiously, like one of the bobbleheads in Matt's collection.

"You seem like you have a good imagination—you have to use it when you read. Reading became fun again when I taught myself to

visualize

visualize the story like a movie. You like movies?"

"Of course I do." I tell her my father is a storyboard artist for films.

"That's perfect. Just picture every paragraph like a scene in a movie. Close your eyes and see the character act out the story in your mind." Margot rummages through her backpack and pulls out a novel.

"I can't read that," I say. "It's too hard."

"You could if you took your time. But it doesn't matter because I'm going to read it to you."

I look up to see Carly staring at Margot and me. She grins and mouths the words *teacher's pet*.

I move away from Margot as if I'm not interested in what she's saying.

But she sees Carly and waves her over. Great.

"Your friend can do this too," Margot says.

"We're not friends!" Carly and I say in unison.

unison

"Close your eyes, both of you."

Carly and I follow Margot's directions, and she reads us part of her book, a scene about a family walking on the beach.

"Picture the ocean," Margot tells us. "Feel how the waves touch your feet. The text said it was a cloudy day—can you picture the clouds?"

I take a peek to see if Carly's eyes are closed; they are. I close mine again and follow the story as Margot describes the main character throwing rocks into the water.

Part of me wonders what the

other kids are doing, but most of me watches the story unfold in my mind. And at the end of the page, when Margot asks us questions about the story, Carly isn't the only one who knows all the answers.

Saying Good-bye to Matt

On my way to Matt's, I run into Joe Brennan at the tennis courts. He waves me over, so I pull my bike to the curb.

"Listen to this," he says. "A chimpanzee who's allergic to bananas—what do you think?"

allergic

I think it's the stupidest thing I've ever heard, but he's got a huge rock in his hand, so I tell him the idea is

tribe

brilliant. He tosses the rock into the air with one hand and catches it with the other.

"So the chimp ends up being the best climber in his tribe because he has to get peanuts instead of bananas."

"Peanuts don't grow on trees." I keep my eye on the rock as I disagree with Joe. "They grow on plants, underground."

"They do not."

"Do, too." What are we, five? I take a few steps away from Joe. "And groups of chimpanzees aren't called tribes. They're called cartloads."

Joe bounces the large rock from one hand to the other even slower than before. "Cartloads of chimpanzees—that doesn't make sense. They can't drive carts."

"Maybe in your story they should. Cartloads of chimpanzees in carts—might be funny." Why am I wasting my time trying to collaborate with this knucklehead?

collaborate

The rock suddenly stops; it appears to weigh a hundred pounds in Joe's meaty hand. "Since when did you get so smart?" he asks.

meaty

"Just 'cuz I have a hard time at school doesn't mean I'm stupid." I skid back and forth on the sidewalk with my bike. "Besides, my mom's a veterinarian. I know a lot about animals."

"'Cuz you *are* one."

I nod as if Joe got the last laugh, but inside I'm thinking, *We're all animals, you moron.* I tell him I'd love to stay and chat—another lie—but I'm on my way to Matt's.

"I might use that cartload of chimps idea," Joe shouts after me. "But I won't give you credit for it!"

As I bike past the school, I think about Pedro. A group of monkeys can also be a cartload, but they can be a barrel too. I wonder when the woman in Venice Beach will bring Pedro back for a checkup. If Pedro wants me to roll him down the street in our recycling barrel with the wheels on it, I'd be happy to oblige.

Matt's family car is loaded with luggage and boxes for their trip. He tells me they will fly from L.A. to Boston, then drive to Cape Cod and take a ferry to Martha's Vineyard. I feel sad for lots of reasons—because my best friend is deserting me, because my family's not going anywhere, and because the rest of

deserting

my summer is going to be WORK, WORK, WORK.

"Learning Camp won't be so bad," Matt says. "Jamie went there when he was our age and said it wasn't that terrible."

"The worst summer of my life!" Jamie jams another bag into the car. "Doing math for an hour, then shooting hoops for ten minutes? That's a formula for misery."

formula

I figure out that Jamie is just helping them pack the car and won't be going on vacation with the rest of the family. His mother gives him instructions ten times about what to do and what not to do while they're gone. I feel bad that he's standing there taking orders from her, but I'm also glad I'm not the only one who gets treated like a kindergartner.

Matt pulls me aside. "First rainy day on the island, I'm going straight to the library."

"You are?" I suddenly feel like I'm alone in protesting the summer reading books.

Matt can read my mind. "Not for the reading list, you goon. I'll see what I can find out about Susan James."

Not only is my best friend leaving, but he's going to be having *my* adventure.

After they pull out of the driveway, Jamie runs into the house and blasts the stereo as loud as it can go. I stand outside for several minutes to see if he'll invite me in, but he doesn't. I ride back home and try to figure out how summer went from being the best season of the year to the absolute total worst.

Susan's Site

My mom has a medical conference on Saturday, so I watch YouTube videos while Dad works. He points to the storyboard he's illustrating and shows me how the director will use it to plan her camera angles and shots.

conference

I know it's a matter of time before he tries to tie the subject into my life, and after a few moments, he does. "Just like the illustrations you do. Have you found them helpful?"

"I do my drawings because they're fun."

I head back to the couch and the laptop. It's Saturday—can I have one day off from learning stuff, please?

I email a quick note to my grandma in Boston, then head for the online Garfield archives. I swear, I don't know what I'd do without him, Calvin, and the other guys. Garfield makes me think about Margot; it's been a week since Carly and I visualized the story with her. Next time I read—whenever that is—I'll definitely do that again. The beach scene we re-created from Margot's book that day reminds me of Susan James, so I type her name into the search engine. After a million other

archives

sites come up, I find a Web page in Susan's memory with photos and quotes from her family.

Staring up from the computer screen is a girl with long brown hair, a huge smile, and a Red Sox cap. In another photo, she holds a field hockey stick with four other athletic girls. I read about what a good student she was, how she helped her neighbors after school, how she loved her younger brother and playing piano. I guess when you're dead no one talks about how you used to fart in bed or talk with your mouth full.

athletic

On the last page is a guestbook. I scroll through the entries and read what her high school classmates and teachers have to say about her. She's been dead for almost a decade, yet

decade

the latest entry was written only a month ago. I guess some people still miss her.

When I look up, I realize I've just spent an hour reading. Part of me is proud of such an accomplishment, but another part wants to protest by jumping on my bike and racing to the pier to watch the guy spray-painted in silver stand like a mannequin for money. The whole time I was reading the entries, a thought kept nagging at me, and now it finally hits the surface. All these people who miss Susan, like her friends Lauren and Danny, miss her because of me.

mannequin

Although no one on this Web site knows I exist, I'm the missing link in their pain. I feel something dark in the center of my chest. I should've figured this day would be a disaster—whoever heard of thinking on a Saturday?

disaster

For several minutes, I face the blank screen, then gather my courage and begin typing my own entry.

Dear Susan,

What were you thinking? You obviously had friends and family who loved you, people more important than some two-year-old you just met. I've seen photos of me at that age; I was cute, but not THAT cute.

I guess what weighs on me most is this: Am I supposed to grow up to be some guy who stops wars or creates new energy sources just because you saved me? Can I still be a normal kid who makes a lot of mistakes, maybe even MORE mistakes than the average kid? I guess what I really want to say is: I didn't ask you to save me, but I'm glad you did.

I hit "enter" and watch my note disappear into time and space.

Movies Run in
the Family

I make a deal with Margot: If I read
the first chapter of one of my
summer reading books, she'll give
all the Mustangs a break and get us
out of Fraction Friday. As much as I
don't want to read one of the books,
I *really* don't want to have some
fake contest with one of the other
camp groups about fractions and
percentages.

percentage

predict

I settle on my bed with Bodi and try the whole movie thing Margot taught Carly and me a few weeks ago. It's harder to do without Margot here, but I take my time, trying to picture every little detail of the story. I even try to predict what might happen in the next scene. I make it halfway through the chapter before I have to take a break.

Bodi puts his front paws on my chest, and I soak in the cool breeze coming from the open windows. I grab my markers and sketchbook and check out all the illustrations I've done so far this summer. As I look through the drawings, I get an idea. I hold the book in one hand and flip through the pages like one of those old flip-o-ramas and suddenly the story of my summer appears like a movie: Mom vaulting over the laundry, me rummaging through the attic.

I feel a little like Carly, eager to find a teacher, because I can't wait to show Margot my vocabulary word flip-o-rama. But there's someone else I have to show first.

eager

Dad is whacking weeds alongside the driveway when I show him my new invention. He pulls off his headphones, wipes the sweat from his hands, and flips through the book himself.

whacking

"I used to make these all the time when I was your age," he says. "I wish I'd thought of it as a way to study vocabulary words. Would've saved Mrs. Patrick from yelling at me all the time."

I wipe the edges of my

sketchbook, which are already smudgy from Dad's hands.

"Makes you really want to get going on that assigned reading and fill the whole book with new words," he says.

contaminated

And just like that, my fun new invention becomes contaminated by work. I go back inside to put away my pad. The attic is steaming hot, but I find the boxes of Christmas ornaments and lights, then get Henry from down the street. We decorate the trees and shrubs in the front yard, even up the trunk of the palm tree near the driveway. I plug the whole thing in, and we sit back and watch the blinking lights.

ornaments

It would make a great scene for my flip-o-rama—if I ever decide to draw again.

A Different
James Bond

It should be illegal to make kids
do math when it's 80 degrees
and sunny and the calendar reads
"August." I wait near the gate for
Mom to pick me up after Prison
Camp and see Carly standing a few
feet away. She spends most of
Learning Camp with three other girls
who practice cheerleading routines
between sessions. We've had a few

illegal

conversations about Ginger the hedgehog but not much else.

When Mom pulls up, I'm surprised to see Carly approach our car.

"What are you doing?" I ask.

My mother answers for her. "Maria called and asked if I could pick up Carly today. By the time we get her back, Maria will be home from work."

Thankfully, Carly doesn't try for the shotgun seat and slides into the back. We haven't even hit the 405 when my mother asks Carly about her summer reading.

"I keep telling Derek he would love one of the books on our list," Carly says. "This boy and his dog meet this guy with a—"

"I worked hard today—can we talk about something else?" I ask.

Carly changes the subject by talking about her mother's landscaping company, and when we get to her house, I see she isn't exaggerating her mother's talents.

exaggerating

Pink hibiscus weaves its way along the fence, and huge bushes of rosemary surround two palm trees on either side of the front door (Carly has to tell me what kinds of plants they are). Even though the smells want to coax me from the car, I still ask my mother if I can wait outside. She says Carly's mom will be home in a minute and insists I come in and wait with Carly.

"This wasn't my idea," Carly whispers as she unlocks the door. "In case you think it was."

Soon Carly's mom pulls up in a small red pickup. She has long, dark hair like Carly's. When Mom accepts an iced green tea from her, I know we'll be here longer than a minute.

Carly asks if I want to see Ginger. I follow her to the dining room, where the hedgehog's crate takes up most of the table. She nibbles at the carrot Carly gives her, then walks to the other side of the cage.

"Can your mom look at her?" Carly asks. "I want to make sure she's okay. She didn't eat much yesterday either."

She hands me a glove—probably one her mother uses to landscape—and I take Ginger out of the crate and hold her like we're back in school.

Mom comes in and examines Ginger. "I haven't seen a hedgehog as a patient in years—I'm not much of an expert. But if you bring her in, I can call a colleague with more experience. It might be the change in location; they hate to be moved."

colleague

Carly nods and I put Ginger back in her cage. My mom and Mrs. Rodriquez head back to the kitchen.

"Hey, do you want to see what I made?" Carly asks.

I tell her sure, but inside I'm thinking, *If this involves dolls, tea parties, or karaoke, I'm grabbing on to that huge spider plant in the living room, smashing through the window, rolling onto the landscaped lawn, and sprinting the whole way home without looking back.*

Carly leads me down to the playroom in the basement. The entire room is laid out in grids of fishing line crisscrossed from floor to ceiling. Because the lines are

invisible

clear, they almost seem invisible. There are at least fifty of them, all fastened to the wall with wide, clear tape.

"You made this?" I ask.

She points to the other side of the room, where a crystal bowl is upside down on top of a stool covered in purple velvet. "I'm pretending this is a famous museum, and that's the largest diamond in the world." She nods toward the fishing line. "This is the alarm system, and I'm a burglar. I have to get to the diamond without triggering any of the motion detectors."

Not that I would ever say so to Carly, but I am *very* impressed. She tosses me a black ski mask and tells me to give it a try. I slip on the mask and limbo under the first line with no problem but nail the second one with my shoulder. I make three more attempts before she asks for a turn.

She puts on the mask, takes a deep breath, and moves across the room like a hybrid gymnast/feline.

hybrid

The image makes me think of Joe Brennan and his stupid fantasy stories. But the person I really want to show this to is Matt. He and I could play this game for hours, hands down.

Carly makes her way under the intricate web of "detectors" until

intricate

she reaches the stool. She bends under the last one like she's going deep underneath a limbo pole, then turns—ever so slowly—to lift the fake diamond into her hands.

I can't help but applaud.

She puts the bowl back on the stool and removes her mask. "I've had a lot of practice," she says. "You want to try again?"

This time, I take off my sneakers before slipping on the mask. When my mother calls down, I ask if we can stay a little longer. She seems surprised but says yes. Carly shows me a few tricks, and by the time we leave an hour later, I've stolen the diamond twice.

I scan the room one last time. "You built this yourself AND read all the summer reading books?"

She shrugs. "It wasn't that hard."

Somehow that just doesn't seem fair. Is that what my summer has come down to—getting my butt kicked by the school's Goody Two-shoes?

A Call from Matt

It's Thursday night, and Amy's favorite show is on, so she basically ignores me while I lie on the floor and rub Bodi's belly. He's back to his old self, but Mom still says he should rest. I wish she'd follow her own advice when it comes to taking care of me.

Amy calls her best friend, Tina, during every commercial and they

celebrity

reaction

ooh and ahh over the celebrity actor playing the doctor on their stupid show. I want to go onto the roof and knock the satellite dish so the picture messes up, but it's raining and Amy's reaction would hardly be worth the effort of getting soaked.

I grab the key and let myself into Mom's office. The receptionist keeps a canister of dog bones on her desk and I grab a few to give to Bodi later. I check to see if Pedro is there, but unfortunately, he's not.

Inside, there are five dogs in large metal cages. They bark when I enter through the swinging door, so I do what I always do to calm them down—give them treats. Then I crawl into one of the empty cages, this time beside the Dalmatian.

As I lie inside the cage, I run my fingers along the metal bars.

It makes me think of the grate at Jamie's store, and I wonder if he's enjoying the rest of the family being gone for a few weeks. Thinking about Jamie makes me miss Matt. It's almost as if remembering Matt makes him remember me because, the next thing I know, Amy's at the door of the office.

"Your friend's on the phone." She tosses me the cordless. "In a cage, perfect—just where you belong."

I grab the phone and tell Matt I was just thinking about him. While he tells me about riding the carousel, kayaking, and eating fish and chips by the harbor at night, I stare at the ceiling of the cage and try not to get depressed at a summer spent playing "baseball math" and drawing pictures of vocabulary words.

"But here's the real news," Matt

carousel

says. "We went to South Beach, the beach where that babysitter saved you from drowning."

I throw one of the bones to the beagle to get him to stop yapping. "What was it like?"

"Monumental waves and a riptide. Could be dangerous for a two-year-old. You were lucky."

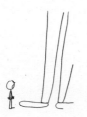

monumental

I press my head against the cool metal of the bars. I can't decide if Susan James was a hero or a knucklehead. Maybe a little bit of both.

"The fair is next week," Matt says. You should talk your mom into coming out for it. It's going to be a blast."

"I'm too busy with multiplication and essays." The beagle wants another treat and starts barking again. I climb out of my cage and make demented faces until she stops.

"So what have you been up to?" Matt asks. "Besides hating Learning Camp."

I tell him the camp counselor for my group isn't so bad. "Plus, she really likes my illustrations."

When Matt asks if I know any of the other kids, I almost tell him Carly attends too but decide against it. If Matt knew I was at her house last week, he'd be on the next plane home to save me.

attends

Matt then tells me about an expert skateboarder he met on the island who taught him several new moves. I'm happy for him but feel a pang of jealousy that he's having more fun with someone else than with me.

"Gotta go," Matt finally says. "Fireworks on the beach tonight."

My summer stinks! Instead of going inside, I climb up the porch to the roof of the garage. Vacation's more than half over, and I haven't done anything fun. This is criminal!

I hear the door and know what to expect.

"Derek!" Amy yells. "Come down this minute or I'll tell your mom you were going through my purse again."

Even though it's still raining, I remove one of my sneakers and pelt it at the satellite dish. Bull's-eye!

Amy shrieks and runs inside to see if I messed up her precious show.

It's not the beach, but at least it's fireworks.

Two Emails

When I get home from camp, there's an email from my grandma saying she can't wait until we visit again. My grandfather died three years ago and now she spends most days bowling with her girlfriends, who are all old but dye their hair and wear big jewelry to pretend they're not. Grandma knows Photoshop even better than my father and every

unfamiliar

email from her includes a funny drawing she made on her computer.

The address of the other email is unfamiliar, but as soon as I read it, I know what it's about.

Derek—

Thanks so much for your entry in our daughter's guestbook. Are you Derek Fallon from California? If so, tell your mother hello. Susan is still very much with us, and it comforts us to know how much she meant to others. I bet you're a wonderful boy and Susan looks down on you from heaven with pride.

Sincerely,
Madeline James

I read the email four times. Why is this woman being so *nice*? If

Susan's watching me from heaven, it's probably with daggers in her eyes thinking about all the fun she's missing down here on earth. It's amazing she doesn't magically appear and push me in front of a train.

I never thought of Susan as some kind of guardian angel; is it possible she's still looking out for me? I stare at my inbox with Mrs. James's note back-to-back with my grandma's. Genius strikes. I head to the kitchen to find my mom.

guardian

"Grandma sure seems lonely," I tell her.

Mom hammers chicken breasts with the pounder to tenderize them for dinner. For someone who dedicates her life to saving animals, she's merciless with the dead ones. "I thought we'd get out to see her

merciless

this summer, but I don't have anyone to cover for me. I feel really guilty about it."

Mom obviously didn't think before she answered. I put my plan into action.

"I hate to go the whole summer without seeing Grandma. I miss her so, so, so much." I wonder if I used too many *so*'s, but Mom puts down the pounder and tilts her head.

"I miss her too," she says. "Let's go out for a nice New England visit this fall."

I wonder if Mom is onto me and is dangling a pull-you-out-of-school trip to shut me up. But I stick to my original plan.

"October is so far away. It's been a year—I really *miss* her."

She stares out the kitchen

window and for once I don't interrupt her silence.

"You're right," she finally says. "I'm going to switch my schedule around. Even a few days with Grandma this summer will be better than no days at all."

I jump up and give Mom a hug. I know I should wait until tonight or maybe even tomorrow before I begin the next phase of the plan, but as usual, my mouth works at a faster speed than my brain. "Maybe while we're back East, we can see Matt."

I'm not sure if it's her veterinary training or just her maternal instincts, but my mother now smells a rat. "Is that what this is about—going to see Grandma because you miss your friend?" When she realizes the second phase of my plan, her face

maternal

flushes with anger. Why wasn't I a little more patient?

"Please tell me this has nothing to do with Susan James."

I insist I'm only thinking about Grandma. "She just sent me an email—she misses me." I make the mistake of pointing to the laptop.

When Mom sees the open email from Susan James's mother, I get a heaping helping of MomMad. It takes several minutes before she stops yelling.

"I *do* miss Grandma. . . . I just thought we could go to Martha's Vineyard too," I admit.

When Mom sends me up to my room, I go. With the laptop.

Just because Mom has ruined my plan doesn't mean I still can't email Grandma to help talk my mother into a visit.

A Truce

The next night, my mother walks into the kitchen with two large pizza boxes. Before I can rip them from her hands, she sits across from me and guards them with her body.

"Okay, here's the deal."

It's difficult to concentrate with the smell of tomato, cheese, and pepperoni, but I try.

"As much as I hate you hatching

secret plans, we do owe Grandma a visit," she says. "So we're all flying to Boston for five days, leaving next Friday. It's the only time I can get Dr. Taylor to cover for me and it's good for Dad too."

"That's great!"

"Dad and I were also trying to take a romantic weekend this summer—"

romantic

"Don't leave me with Amy!"

"Calm down. We decided to all go back East instead."

I gather up my courage for the next question because I have to know. "Can we go to Martha's Vineyard? To see Matt, I mean."

"I already spoke to Matt's mother. They're flying back after the fair, so they won't be there."

I'm a little sad about not going

to the Scene of the Crime with my best friend, but three days off from Learning Camp, a plane ride, and seeing my grandma are all reasons to celebrate.

Mom pulls out another bit of unexpected news. "We're going to the Vineyard anyway," she says. "You've been so curious about Susan all summer. We'll go to South Beach, even visit Susan's mom. That way you can see there's no big mystery and move on."

I jump up and down with excitement before I realize there has to be a catch. There's *always* a catch.

"But you have to work on the school reading list so we don't spend the rest of the summer arguing about it."

negotiate

Before I say "deal," I decide to negotiate. "Can Bodi come with us?"

She shakes her head. "I think Bodi should stay at Pet Camp, don't you?"

When I stand toe-to-toe with her, I can't wait till we're both the same height—maybe that will make these discussions a little more fair. I look her in the eye and try one last plea. "He's part of the family. He should come."

She thinks about this for a moment. "It *is* always more of a family vacation with Bodi. Deal." She pushes one of the pizza boxes toward me. "This one's all yours."

I tear open the box, but instead of a large pepperoni and cheese, I find three of the books from my summer reading list, including the one Ms. Williams gave me that I haven't read since Dad contaminated my flip-o-rama book. (Mom is *really* good at finding stuff.) She tries not to laugh, then points upstairs.

A third of a pizza is much less fun than one all to yourself, but I'm starving and open the other box. I take a slice and rip a paper towel from the roll and head up to my room.

"Aren't you forgetting something?" Mom asks.

I grab Ms. Williams's book from the pizza box—it'll make a good plate—then plop down on my bed. For the first time, I notice the notes Ms. Williams made in the margins. *What is the main character feeling? What do you think could happen next?* Her notes raise questions of my own. *How long will it take to read*

*a book if I have to stop every minute
to answer these stupid questions?*

I shove the book under my mattress and do something easier: email Grandma to tell her how happy I am that we're coming to Boston.

What Are You Doing Here?

I keep Bodi on the leash when I take him for his morning walk, even though I know he'd love to chase a few squirrels. I used to let him off-leash, but my mother just treated a Lab that got hit by a car, and it was *not* a pretty sight. When we reach the lot near the recreation field, Bodi takes a leak and I do too. I find a shady spot under a large beech, and

recreation

aroma

Bodi sneaks in next to me. He ran through a stream on our way here and now he has that wet-dog smell. It's my favorite aroma on the planet so I bury my face in his fur.

Across the field, a group of women are playing softball. I ignore them and reach for my book. I suddenly realize I'm reading a comic where Calvin leans against a tree with Hobbes next to him in the exact same position Bodi and I are in. Weird.

"Derek Fallon, is that you?"

I look up to see Ms. Williams running over from first base. She's wearing a Red Hot Chili Peppers tank top and high-top sneakers, and her hair's in pigtails. I try to pretend I'm someone else and hide behind Bodi, but she's already across the field.

"How's your summer going?"

I can't look her in the eye. She's wearing cut-off jeans and has a tattoo of a dove on her shoulder that I've never noticed. I feel like running home. Fast.

I mumble something about having a stinky summer.

She points to my Calvin and Hobbes book. "I see you're reading. That's not stinky." She bends down to pet Bodi who slobbers all over Ms. Williams's face. But instead of backing away, she lets Bodi cover her with kisses and talks to him in the same stupid baby-voice my mother uses with every animal, even though she's a professional. If some moron like Joe Brennan is across the field watching Ms. Williams make out with my dog, I will never hear the end of it.

"I found the notes you wrote

slobber

in the margins of the book you gave me."

"Were they helpful?"

"A little." I take my sketchbook out of my pack and show her the flip-o-rama movie of my summer so far.

She sits next to me on the grass and goes through the book herself. "I got an email from Carly saying you've been doing some great drawings this summer—I guess she was right."

Carly sends emails to teachers? During vacation? What a FREAK! I am forever grateful to the pitcher who yells, "Annie! You're up!"

Ms. Williams heads back to her position, calling over her shoulder for me to enjoy the rest of the summer. If she weren't my teacher, she would almost seem cool. I inhale Bodi's aroma one more time and try to return to my book, but I can't. Carly emails Ms. Williams? She said my drawings were great? I wonder why she never told me?

When I get home, there are three emails waiting from Grandma saying how excited she is for our visit and asking if I want her to cook any special meals. I email her back and tell her I can't wait to see her too. I also happen to mention barbecued chicken, mashed potatoes, and chocolate cake with coconut frosting.

I know my mom would be mad, but the next site I go to is Susan James's guestbook. I've read these entries several times already, but the ones by Lauren Hutchins are funny and nice. Reading her entries, I find out she was with Susan at the beach that day. No one said anything about Susan being with a friend! I decide not to say anything to Mom in case she thinks I'm obsessed and cancels our trip.

I type Lauren's name into the search engine and learn she has a jewelry stall in an artists' gallery in Chilmark, which just happens to be on Martha's Vineyard. The photo shows silver bracelets and glass beads displayed in bowls of uncooked rice. On the "About Me" page, Lauren looks around the same age as Ms. Williams. I write down her store address on the inside cover of the book I'm supposed to be reading. Seeing Ms. Williams today makes me feel a tiny bit guilty about blowing off my reading yet again. Instead, I try to decide what would be more fun:

a) spray my father's shaving cream around Bodi's mouth

displayed

and run around the neighborhood pretending he has rabies
or

rabies

b) get Henry to loan me his
   headgear, tie it on Bodi, and
   attach a stuffed animal to the
   front so he can chase it like
   a greyhound running after a
   rabbit.

Both ideas seem fun, but my
markers are calling. My hand hovers
over the case—deep blue? Orangey
brown? I choose the lime green,
grab a handful of cookies from the
cupboard, and head for the porch to
draw.

Monkey See,
Monkey Do

yoga

The medicine my mother ordered for Pedro comes in, and she plans on dropping it off before her yoga class. When I beg her to let me see Pedro again, she says I can come with her.

I thought Mom's friend Debbie was the one who had Pedro as a companion, but it turns out to be her son, Michael. He's seventeen years old, has cerebral palsy, and is in a wheelchair. Pedro has been with Michael for two years; they're best friends. I'm kind of envious. Matt is great, but he's no monkey.

While Mom tells Debbie about her conference, Michael wheels around the large, open apartment with Pedro on his lap. There's a basketball hoop on its lowest setting outside Michael's bedroom, and we shoot hoops to twenty-one. Michael kicks my butt.

When we're done, Michael picks up a laser pointer and aims it at the tall case of DVDs. Pedro jumps from Michael's lap, removes the correct DVD from the rack, and places it in the player. Then Pedro hurries to the kitchen, opens the cupboard, takes out a bag of popcorn, and puts it in the microwave. It's everything

laser

I hoped hanging out with a monkey would be.

"The organization that trained Pedro is always looking for foster homes," Michael says. "Your mom's a vet—I bet you'd have a good chance of getting one."

I now have a new and exciting mission: talking my mother into letting us raise a monkey.

When Mom says it's time to go, I ask if I can watch a movie with Michael instead of tagging along with her to the yoga studio. Debbie says that's fine, so Mom agrees to pick me up in an hour and a half.

Pedro gets a bottle of water from the fridge and places it in the holder on Michael's chair. Pedro's little face seems almost human and anyone can see he's looking at Michael with affection. I never really thought about my mom choosing veterinary medicine as a career, but for the first time I realize how cool it is to dedicate your life to helping little guys like Pedro and Bodi.

affection

As we watch the movie, I remember this is one Dad worked on a few years ago. When the chase scene comes on, I tell Michael how my father drew storyboards for it. The scene is full of suspense and fast camera work. Michael yells at the screen for the main character to watch out, but all I think about is how both my parents are really good at what they do. Am I ever going to be that good at anything? Maybe I'm not even their child; maybe they found me on the boardwalk, felt bad for me, and took me home.

Pedro must be a supermonkey who can read people's feelings because he inches away from Michael toward me. He sits between us, and when the car chase sequence ends, I'm back to my old self.

Afterward, I show Michael my sketchbook. "They're not as good as my father's drawings," I explain. "I'm still learning."

Michael spins his wheelchair toward the computer station in the corner and tells me to bring my book. "You should animate those drawings," he says. He opens a folder on his computer and asks me to drag over a chair.

Next to the keyboard, there's a flat pad that Michael tells me to draw on. As if by magic, what I draw on the pad appears on the screen. Then

Michael manipulates the lines on my drawing until they start to move.

"You're turning my illustration into a real cartoon—that's amazing!"

manipulates

By the time Mom comes back from yoga class, Michael and I have animated several of my vocabulary words. At the beginning of the summer, I learned how to picture a story as if it's a movie in my head. Now, thanks to Michael, that movie isn't in my head anymore. It's like my flip-o-rama book just jumped onto the computer screen for all to see.

Both my mother and Michael's love what we've done and agree that Michael and I can get together again as soon as we come back from the Vineyard. When Mom and I leave, Pedro jumps into my arms to say good-bye.

The entire ride home, I ask Mom if we can be a foster home for a capuchin like Pedro. Mom finds a million new ways to say no. She tells Dad about the work Michael and I did on his computer and Dad gets excited. He says he's been avoiding that kind of animation software for his work, but I've inspired him to investigate some programs after we get back.

inspired

As I pack my markers and sketchbook in my roller suitcase, I almost feel like I helped Dad with something important. Maybe he can return the favor by helping me talk Mom into getting a monkey.

Grandma

My mother wears an eye mask for most of the flight to Boston; she gets nervous on planes and usually just wants the journey to be over. At least she's not worried about Bodi— she was one of the vets hired by the airline to come up with a plan to make it comfortable for pets to fly. Because of that, Bodi always travels for free.

My father and I play cards and watch a movie. After that, I roam up and down the aisles until a flight attendant suggests I take my seat. When I ask if I can go below to visit Bodi, she tells me passengers aren't allowed in the cargo area. Then she gets all sappy and asks if I miss Bodi, if he's "boy's best friend" and all this other mushy stuff. I ask her for a little can of pineapple juice and go back to my seat.

cargo

It takes a while before Bodi's crate comes off the plane. He relieves himself the second we get outside. We rent a car that smells much newer than ours back home and drive to Grandma's.

Grandma still lives in the same house my mother grew up in, but now all Mom's horse ribbons and Beatles posters are in the basement and her old bedroom is an exercise room. Whenever we visit, I sleep on a blow-up mattress next to the treadmill.

"Where is he? Where's my boy?" Grandma hurries down the driveway and starts to hug me before I'm even out of the car.

Mom and Dad smile at each other; I guess grandparent love is a different thing than parent love. My parents seem glad to let someone else make a fuss over me for a while.

Grandma squeezes me like she hasn't seen me in a century, even though it's been only a year. When I spot a chocolate cake with shredded coconut waiting on the kitchen counter, I hug her back even harder.

Grandma has her hearing aids in today so we don't have to scream

1909—2009

century

like we usually do. She plays us a DVD of her bowling team's highlights and shows us the "killer roll" that helped bring her team to the finals. When my mother asks if she wants to come with us to the Vineyard, Grandma says she'd love to but can't disappoint her teammates. She lets me play with my uncle's old crutches and tells stories of how my mother used to try to heal all the sick animals in the neighborhood. We smile and laugh when she takes out pictures of Mom and her brother when they were kids, even though we've seen them dozens of times before.

Unlike our house, where everyone takes care of themselves, here Grandma waits on us like we're special company and I guess we are. She treats me the same way she did when I was little, offering to rub

disappoint

my feet. I let her, happy to be a little kid again, even if it's just for a short time.

As I'm sitting on her lap—spilling out of the chair because I'm as tall as she is—I get an idea. "Grandma, will you read me a story?"

"I'd LOVE to," she answers.

I run to my bag and get the summer reading book that was part of the deal to come here.

"Oh no," Mom says. "You're reading that one on your own."

"No, I want to!" Grandma moves to the couch and puts on her reading glasses. "This looks like a good story."

My parents' glares can't dim the huge grin on my face as I snuggle with my grandmother. Mom tries to get us to play Pictionary instead, but I ask Grandma to keep reading. Mom

glare

and Dad finally give up and go for a walk around the neighborhood with Bodi.

When Grandma winks at me, I'm not sure if it's because she's glad we're visiting or because she knows she's bailing me out of my work. As she reads, I use Margot's technique and visualize the character. Is he feeling guilty? Nervous? I imagine the house he's sitting in, with its blue rug and large clock on the wall. By the time my parents come back, Grandma and I have finished two chapters.

Our bodies are still on West Coast time, so my parents and I stay up after Grandma goes to bed and watch a movie.

With any luck, I can get Grandma to help write my report too.

Martha's Vineyard

We spend several days with Grandma, watching her bowl, meeting her friends, and eating more desserts than even I thought was humanly possible. Matt almost succeeded in talking his parents into meeting us at Grandma's for an afternoon before they fly to L.A., but his father had to get back for a meeting. Matt and I talk on the phone and can't believe

friends

spine

we're both in Massachusetts but have to wait till we're back home to hang out again.

When we leave, Grandma hugs me so hard I'm afraid my spine will break in half. Mom tries again to talk her into coming with us, but Grandma is committed to her tournament and says she'll be out to see us for Thanksgiving. As we drive to the ferry, I can tell Mom already misses her.

My father is excited the ferry has wireless Internet, so he settles into a booth with a cup of coffee and his laptop. Mom and I stroll the deck with Bodi, who stops to sniff the butt of every other dog heading to Vineyard Haven. We check out passengers as they walk by—a six-foot-tall guy in a Patriots jersey who's carrying his wife's floral suitcase, a woman feeding fried clams to a toddler wearing a Cape Cod T-shirt. When the guy next to us makes a loud business call on his cell, Mom makes a gun with her index finger and thumb and pretends to shoot it out of his hand. I love it when Mom's in vacation mode.

floral

Her mood changes, however, when we drive off the ferry. We're behind a large SUV loaded with four bikes and two kayaks, and I realize people come here for reasons other than exploring their past. Mom must be thinking the same thing; she and Dad haven't been to the Vineyard since that fateful trip ten years ago. She seems less animated and fun when she gives my father directions to the pet-friendly bed-and-breakfast she found online.

fateful

I eye the four-poster bed, but my parents shoot me looks that say, *Don't even think about jumping on that.* I beg them to open up the pullout couch so I can see where I'm going to sleep, but Mom wants to explore the island and Dad wants to get some lunch. We leave Bodi in the room with a rawhide bone and walk to town.

The three of us browse through bookstores, my parents' favorite thing to do on vacation. I go to the back of the store and hide behind one of the shelves. I know I'm too old for picture books—OBVIOUSLY!—but I can't help paging through them. When my mother heads toward me, I toss the book back and grab the nearest chapter book.

"Would you like that one?" Her

voice is filled with so much hope, I almost say yes.

I answer no but tell her there's a fudge shop next door. I'm finally rewarded for my patience with a marshmallow-crispy-rice-almond-coconut fudge square.

We go back to the bed-and-breakfast to get Bodi before we go exploring. As we drive from one town to the next, I don't feel as if we're on an island. It's more like rolling farms, old stone walls, and lots of scrubby trees. Nothing here reminds me of California. The public beach is lined with cars with license plates from all over the country, but my mother knows a secret beach, so we wave good-bye to the crowds and head farther south.

When I see a large barn with the

sign CHILMARK ARTISTS, I realize this is where Lauren Hutchins sells her jewelry.

"STOP!" I scream.

My father skids to a halt and tells me I almost gave him a heart attack. I point to the wooden sign. "I thought it said HOMEMADE ICE CREAM."

Dad shakes his head sadly. "I'm not sure Learning Camp has even dented your reading issues."

"Might as well take a look while we're here." Mom grabs her purse and crosses the street.

anxious

As excited as I am, I'm also anxious. Suppose Lauren Hutchins isn't here today? Even worse, suppose she *is* here, recognizes me as the kid who killed her best friend, and becomes a raging lunatic? Worse than *that*, suppose *nothing* happens and I've spent my summer obsessed with something that doesn't have any meaning at all.

As we walk toward the large barn, I wish I were doing anything else—even reading. I slip the leash on Bodi and bring him along for good luck.

Tongue-tied

fleece

dreadlocks

As Dad checks out leatherbound notebooks, Mom tries on handmade fleece jackets. I quietly make my way from booth to booth until I see Hutchins Designs. I pull Bodi behind a tall CD rack made of twigs and check out Lauren Hutchins. Her long brown hair is in dreadlocks, tied back with a large woven scarf. She wears yoga pants and a tie-dyed hoodie. Her earrings are made with feathers and tiny silver beads; several variations of the same design fill the display case beside her. Before I can assess the situation, she spots Bodi.

"Come here, fella. Come on." She bends down and gestures to Bodi, who immediately goes to her. When I stop hating girls and start wanting to date them—twenty or thirty years from now—I'm definitely taking lessons from Bodi. My dog makes out with more pretty girls than any hunky doctor on TV.

"What's his name?" Lauren asks.

"Bodi."

She continues to scratch his head and eventually looks up at me. "You here to buy a present for your girlfriend?"

Her ridiculous comment makes

me even more nervous than I already am. I tell her no and pretend to look at the jewelry. I pick up a leather necklace with shells and a few feathers.

"Feathers are good luck, did you know that? Birds were considered messengers from the gods."

messenger

For the life of me, I can't spit out one word that makes sense. When she points to my T-shirt and asks if I skateboard, all I can do is nod yes. To make matters worse, my father strolls over, quietly checking out Lauren's work as if he's some kind of jewelry expert. *Please go,* I want to say. *This is hard enough without you here.* To complicate things, my mother comes by too.

complicate

"Did you and Bodi find a new friend?" My mother smiles at Lauren as she checks out her wares.

wares

I want to cover myself in one of the woven blankets in the next stall and hide until our vacation is over. Lauren looks at each of us with an expression of friendly confusion, as if she's trying to figure out who we are and why we're there. *I read your guestbook entry,* I want to say. *We were both there when Susan James died.* My scheme to tie up this summer mystery now seems like a giant mistake. When my parents move to the pottery display down the aisle, I follow along behind them. I glance over to see Lauren Hutchins one more time, but she's helping an elderly woman try on a bracelet and doesn't look up.

Back in the car, my father makes my mother feel the soft leather cover of the new sketchbooks he bought for both of us. I sit in the backseat and fume about how I just blew my big chance with Lauren. I gather all the strength I have and tell my parents a straight-out lie.

"I left my book inside," I say.

"You took it in with you?" my mother asks.

"Yes, and I left it on one of the tables. I'll be right back." I jump out of the car and hope for one last chance at hearing Lauren's story firsthand.

The Truth Is Never
What You Think

When I race back to Lauren's stall, she's sitting on a stool, reading. I take a deep breath and dive in.

"I saw your entry on Susan James's Web site," I begin.

She tilts her head. "What? You knew Susan?"

I stand there for several moments waiting for words to emerge. "I was with her at the beach when she died," I finally say.

emerge

She puts down her book and gets off the stool. "How old are you?" She touches my hair as if I'm an alien life-form.

"Twelve," I say.

"That would be about right." She looks into my eyes as if she's trying to conjure up that boy from a decade ago. "That remains the worst day of my life. Susan was my best friend."

Lauren suddenly makes the connection. "What did you do—track me down online?"

I tell her I just found the newspaper article about the drowning this year, that my mother told me what she knew but I wanted to know more.

"You don't have to tell me anything if it's too painful," I add. Just because *I* want to hear more, it might be hard for Lauren—probably as difficult as

conjure

I've made this for Mom all summer. Thinking of Mom makes me realize I only have a few minutes before they come looking for me. *Lauren, hurry!*

Lauren plays with the tips of her hair as she talks. "You have to remember that Susan was a teenager, only a few years older than you are now. She had a crush on this guy—Tim Jensen. He didn't even know she existed, but she used to talk about him all the time. She wanted me to meet her at the beach where she knew he was going to be. When I got there, I couldn't believe she had a kid with her!"

I point to myself and Lauren nods.

"She never mentioned anything about babysitting, and that part of the beach isn't good for little

anticipation

fearless

kids, especially after a storm. But when Tim and his friends came by, Susan wasn't watching you, believe me." Lauren gets up to help a man look for a hair clip for his wife. The anticipation of my parents walking in almost makes my head explode.

"I was playing in the sand with you," Lauren finally continues. "You were one fearless little boy." Lauren's eyes darken, and she sits back down on the stool. "When I turned around, Susan was in the water with Tim and his friends. I mean, she just left you there."

Just as I think I'm going to burst if I don't hear the rest of the story, someone behind me coughs. My parents and Bodi are now standing in the booth.

Before they can ask why I lied

about losing the book, I introduce them to Lauren Hutchins. "She was Susan's best friend," I say. "She was with her the day of the accident."

My mother looks like she's just been shot out of a cannon. I know when we leave I'm in for the biggest portion of MomMad ever.

portion

"You and I looked for shells on the beach while Susan and Tim went for a walk," Lauren continues. "After he left, Susan was just so happy. She and I tried to make a sand castle with you, but all you wanted to do was run around."

Sounds familiar.

"Even though the waves were huge, Susan insisted on going for a swim. She loved the water, always did. We were way over on the right, past where the lifeguards sit. She wasn't in the water for a minute before the undertow got a hold of her. I'm not a strong swimmer, so I ran to get help."

My mother seems almost as shocked and tongue-tied as I am. "Susan wasn't trying to save Derek?"

Lauren shook her head. "The only time he was near the water was after the ambulance came. It was so busy, no one saw him wander in." She reaches over and tousles my hair again. "Lucky for you, your dog grabbed your diaper and pulled you back to shore."

tousles

I can't remember one time when my family has ever said anything in unison, but we do now. "Bodi?!"

When everyone in the barn looks over to Lauren's stall, she bursts out laughing, then bends down to Bodi and kisses him all over again. "He must've been only a few years old, but he was fearless too."

My mother looks like she's going to pass out. "The woman from the service said Susan was trying to save Derek. Susan's mother said that too."

"Watching your best friend die is one of the worst things you can possibly experience," Lauren says. "But having to lie about it after made it so much worse."

My mother asks her to explain.

"When I couldn't see Susan in the water, I started screaming, picked up Derek, and ran to get help. Two guys dove into the water while I went to the parking lot to call Susan's mother—this was before cell phones. Mrs. James got here right away. She was absolutely hysterical. When the

hysterical

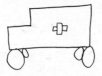
ambulance

ambulance arrived and the police asked what happened, she took over and said Susan was trying to save the child she was babysitting."

Lauren inhaled deeply and started to cry. "I'm still not sure if she misunderstood me or just assumed that Susan was being heroic, but she was so crazy with fear, I went along with her. I wanted to tell the police the truth, but I was young and Mrs. James was so upset. When the police questioned me later, it just seemed easier to stick with Mrs. James's story."

A giant wave of relief washes over my mother. She didn't do anything wrong by hiring a new babysitter, her son didn't cause someone's death, there was nothing to ask forgiveness for. As for me, I still felt bad that Susan died but in a different, less responsible way.

"I tried a few times over the years to tell other people what really happened," Lauren adds, "but I couldn't. It makes me sad Susan's mother rushed to an assumption and insisted on some ideal version of Susan that never existed. Everyone on the island still thinks Susan died a hero."

My mother sits on the stool and doesn't talk for a long while. When she finally whispers to my father, I overhear what she says.

"All these years Madeline led me to believe her daughter died saving Derek. I can't believe this! It's an outrage!"

outrage

I squeeze in next to my mom. "It wasn't my fault—that's good news, right? You should be happy."

My father agrees and tells Mom they can talk about it later. Even though she's upset, she thanks Lauren and buys some jewelry, almost like she's paying her back for finally giving her the truth.

Mom is crying as she hugs Lauren good-bye. When we get ready to leave, Lauren grabs me.

"This is a gift." She holds out the leather necklace with the shells and feathers I was looking at earlier. "Wear it when you skateboard."

"Maybe it'll bring me a message from the gods."

She smiles. "Sometimes all you can hope for is a good ride." She fastens it around my neck, then holds me out to admire the necklace. I take her words and her feathers as a kind of all-weather gear to wrap around me in a storm.

I hug Lauren good-bye even

though I don't have to, then catch
up to my parents. They're standing
beside the car, and my mom's still
crying.

betrayed

"We're going to visit Madeline
James a day early," she says. "I feel
so betrayed. This time *I'm* the one
who wants some answers."

My father shoots me an
expression that says, *Look what
you've gotten us into now.*

Mrs. James

reconsider

When my father asks my mother to reconsider, her answer is an outburst of anger and hurt. I'd give anything to rewind to the day I found that newspaper article. *What was I thinking?*

Mrs. James's house is surrounded by roses, and I suddenly wonder how Carly's doing at Learning Camp. And just like our visit to Carly's, I ask my mother if I can wait in the car.

"You started this," my mom says. "You might as well see how it ends."

Mrs. James meets us in the garden. She's wearing green boots, tan shorts, and a bright pink shirt. Even though her hair is very blond, she looks much older than my parents. "I didn't expect you until tomorrow! But please come in."

She seems touched to finally meet us and gives my mother a hug. Mom wears the same pinched expression she has when my uncle Bob visits with a new girlfriend.

Mrs. James bends down to shake my hand. "And you must be Derek. Let's get you some lemonade."

We follow her to the kitchen, where she takes a pitcher from the fridge. The half slices of lemon float in the container like sunny smiles; I wonder if they'll change to frowns after Mom gives Mrs. James a piece of her mind. Even though Mrs. James lied all those years about the facts of her daughter's death, I pray Mom doesn't let her see the anger she displayed in the car. My father looks as worried as I do.

The walls are filled with unframed photos of Susan in a giant collage that reminds me of the photos of patients in Mom's office. I tug Mom's sleeve and point to the collage, but her mind is focused on this decade-long injustice.

injustice

"Susan would've been twenty-eight next week." Mrs. James runs her finger with its bright pink nail across the photo of her daughter holding a cat.

"About that day—" my mother begins.

Mrs. James turns toward my mother, and the earth stops spinning on its axis—or at least that's how it seems to me. Mrs. James's eyes are filled with such sadness, they actually halt the words coming out of my mother's mouth. No matter what Mrs. James made up about Susan's heroism, the woman lost her daughter, and judging by the look in her eyes, it might as well have been yesterday.

I've never seen my mom struggle the way she does now. She stares at her feet, shakes her head, and after a few moments, looks up.

"Susan sounds like a wonderful girl," Mom says. "Please tell us more."

And just like that, Mrs. James's face lights up, and she shows us pictures of Susan at her dance

axis

recital

sacrifice

official

recital, Susan with her grandparents in Germany, Susan and the child she tutored after school. No one interrupts her and we nod with enthusiasm as Mrs. James goes from photo to photo. My mother puts her arm on mine for just a second, then turns her attention back to Mrs. James. In all the movies I've watched, I don't think I've seen anyone make a bigger sacrifice than Mom makes today. When we leave a few hours later, my mother and Mrs. James hug for a long time.

As we pull out of the driveway, my mom stares out the window. "Are we done with the story of Susan James?" she finally asks.

"It's official. That story is closed," I say. "But there's a new one that needs our immediate attention."

When she turns in her seat to

face me, she's smiling. "And what's that?"

"When do we eat?"

Mom tries to grab me, but I slide across the seat toward Bodi.

"I guess Mom picked the right dog when she rescued Bodi from the shelter all those years ago," Dad says.

I nod but the truth is that Lauren's story doesn't make me love Bodi more. Not because I don't appreciate that he saved my life, but because it's impossible for me to love him one bit more than I already do. I'm his Calvin and he's my Hobbes—always has been, always will be.

Bodi lies on my lap, belly up, and I rub him vigorously. "You had my diaper in your mouth, you dirty dog. I hope it wasn't full of poop." He meets my eyes as if to say, *I would've saved you anyway, you big knucklehead.*

One More Thing

The next day, something is bothering me, but I can't figure out what. As my parents read the paper and drink coffee on the porch, I realize what's been nagging at me.

"Okay, I know I said the story of Susan James is officially closed, but there's one more thing we have to do before we leave the island."

My father's head drops like he's

been hit in the back of the neck with a basketball. My mother ignores me and keeps reading.

"We have to go to South Beach. It's where it all happened."

"Too many memories," Dad says. "Not to mention crowded."

"How about if we go early?" I ask. "Just for a few minutes. Please?"

My mother puts down her newspaper. "Does it ever end?"

"Yes. Today, I promise."

Margot's way of visualizing a book as if it's a movie, my flip-o-rama drawings, and Michael's animation of my vocabulary words have sort of changed the way I think about stories. Not seeing South Beach when we're on Martha's Vineyard seems like a missing frame in the life of Susan James.

My mother is silent for several minutes. "I actually think it's a good idea. Let's go now before it gets too hot."

"And crowded," my dad says again.

disregarded

I ask if Bodi can come, but Mom says dogs aren't allowed on the beach during summer hours. Lucky for me, Susan James disregarded those rules ten years ago.

We pack water bottles, sunscreen, and snacks, and head across the island.

Dad parks along the side of the road and we walk to the right where Lauren said she and Susan went that day. Walking so far in the deep sand is difficult, so we move to the shoreline, where the packed wet sand makes it easier.

After we pass the last lifeguard,

we go on for several minutes more.
The waves are bigger than other
beaches we've been to on this
trip; I actually jump at the noise one
of them makes when it crashes
beside me.

My father grabs my mother's
hand, and we keep walking. After a
while, my parents stop and face the
water. The landscape is beautiful,
but it's hard not to think about what
happened here. I take a deep breath
and say good-bye to Susan James.
Mom grabs my hand; the ocean view
is infinite.

infinite

"Next stop, Portugal," my father
says.

I throw some rocks into the
water and think about Mrs. James
struggling to go through daily
activities like weeding her garden
or taking out the trash because of

a bad decision her daughter made all those years ago. I'm certainly not the only one who'd want to rewind back to that day and make some different choices. Thankfully, I'm spared from all this thinking when my mother's cell goes off with its Pink Panther ringtone.

She turns away from the water to take the call, and I can tell by her face something's wrong. Has something happened to Bodi or Grandma or Matt or Michael or Pedro?

I jump in circles around Mom when I hear her say, "I'm so sorry."

She holds out her hand for me to stop disturbing her so she can hear. I turn toward the ocean where the postcard view seems ominous again.

"What happened?" I ask when my mother says good-bye.

"That was Carly's mom. They

disturbing

ominous

found Ginger dead in her cage this morning. Carly feels terrible—she's very upset."

I'm relieved it's the class hedgehog instead of someone I love. Then I realize Carly probably feels awful even though she only had Ginger for the summer. When a giant wave comes, it hits my legs and I feel the tug of the riptide, the same undertow that pulled Susan James away from her life. I borrow Mom's phone and pull up the number of the last call received.

When Mrs. Rodriquez answers, I ask if I can speak to Carly. I can tell she's crying when she finally comes to the phone.

"It's not your fault," I say. "You didn't do anything wrong."

I sit in the sand and listen, caught between the waves and Carly's sobs.

As Good as It Gets

Often when we take family vacations, we have busy schedules: hiking, seeing friends, visiting museums. But for the rest of this trip we do nothing, and it's a hundred times better. When I tell my parents, they agree.

For my Mom, SUSAN JAMES DROWNING ON HER OWN + ME BEING ALIVE = LESS STRESS FOR EVERYONE

INVOLVED. She lets me eat fish and chips wrapped in paper and doesn't wipe the tartar sauce off my chin. She just laughs when I ask if I can run through the golf course in my underwear at night. It's almost as if that newspaper article had taken root in a small corner of my mother's brain and finding out what really happened has somehow dissolved that tiny growth, freeing Mom up for other things.

dissolved

For our last day, Mom wants to go to Lambert Cove to see the sunset. It's a beach for town residents, but after six o'clock, anyone can go. We park our car, leave our shoes alongside everyone else's, and walk down the wooden, sandy boardwalk to the beach. My dad identifies plants as we go and stops to make

residents

a few notes when he gets an idea. I know Bodi wants to be off-leash, but I also know Mom's enjoying it here and I don't want to ruin her fun by breaking the rules. (For once.)

I bend down and see droplets of water on a spiderweb between two shrubs. I have to agree with Mom when she says this place is magical. When we finally reach the water, I understand why she loves it so much. It's one of the most beautiful beaches I've ever seen, completely different from those back home.

"Why don't you take Bodi off the leash?" Mom says. "I'm sure he wants to run."

She doesn't have to ask twice. Even though he runs slower than he did when I was little, Bodi almost keeps up with me. When I turn back to find my parents, they're walking arm in arm far behind.

A few younger kids are playing Frisbee near the dunes while their grandfather cooks hamburgers on a small grill. The smell attracts Bodi, who sniffs around the man's cooler.

attracts

"You want a burger?" he asks me. "There's more than enough to go around."

Even though I've eaten fish and chips, two chocolate cookies, a strawberry smoothie, and a bag of pretzels, I say yes. The man tells me to help myself to the ketchup, mustard, and relish from his cooler.

"Oops!" The man pretends to drop a burger in the sand, then gives it to Bodi. I think about doing one of my classics where I squirt ketchup on my hand and tell my parents I cut

squirt

myself on a fishhook, but they look so happy I decide to let them be.

I might've seen an East Coast sunset when I was little, but I certainly don't remember anything like the oranges and pinks that fill the sky now. I stand still for several minutes and feel a kind of joy. Then the moment passes—like all perfect moments do—and the imperfect ones roll in like waves. A mosquito nails me on the ankle and the bite swells to the size of a nickel. I drop the last piece of hamburger in the sand and a lady yells at me to put Bodi back on his leash. It's okay, though; anyone who expects perfect to stick around is a moron.

The four of us sit in the sand and watch the sky until after the sun is long gone. I pick up Bodi's poop in a plastic bag and am surprised when we get to the parking lot and there aren't any trash barrels. My mom says it's "Take Out What You Bring In," so I find a place in the trunk where the bag won't get squished.

We spent so much time at the beach that we have to hurry to make the ferry. Mom drives since she knows the island better than Dad does. When we pull into the large boat, the attendant yells at my mother in a Boston accent I've only heard on TV.

accent

"Hey, lady!" he shouts. "Pay attention! Over here!"

I love it when her MomMad isn't directed at me. "Did he just call me 'lady'?" she asks. "Did he?"

My father tells her it's no big deal, but I can see the anger rising in my mother's eyes. The guy motions furiously for my mother to drive forward until our car almost touches the one in front of us.

"Excuse me?" she asks. "But did you have to be so rude?"

"Lady, I've got to move a ton of cars through here in the next few minutes. Don't take it personal."

"Personally," she corrects him.

I almost feel bad for the guy, but not quite.

We decide to sit in the upper cabin and grab supplies from the car for the crossing.

"Aren't you forgetting something?" Dad asks.

I find the bag of Bodi's poop and while the attendant directs cars onto the ferry I drop it into the tiny workroom where he'll hang out during our voyage. Both Mom and

Dad see me, but instead of being angry, they both laugh. As we head upstairs, we can already smell the fumes.

It's almost another perfect moment.

Back Home

arrival

Ten minutes after our arrival, Matt skateboards over to my house. After listening to Lauren Hutchins talk about losing her best friend, I'm happier than usual to see Matt walk in the door.

We skateboard down to the boardwalk, and I tell Matt all about Lauren, Mrs. James, and South Beach. When I tell him Bodi saved my life and not Susan, he suggests we contact the mayor and try to get an official Bodi Holiday so we can take a day off from school. He also tells me Jamie had to pay a professional service a week's salary to clean up the monumental mess he made in the house before their parents came home. We order strawberry slushies and watch the high school kids surf around the rocks. It's amazing how different two oceans can be.

As we ride home, I tell Matt we have to make a stop. When he asks where we're going, I say we have to play superhero and lend assistance to someone in need. He seems okay with that until he sees the name RODRIQUEZ on the door.

assistance

"Is this Carly's house? Dude, what are we *doing* here?" he whispers.

"We're helping Carly plant some flowers for Ginger."

"Miss Goody Two-shoes killed the class hedgehog?" A demented grin appears on Matt's face until he sees my expression.

"She's not that bad," I say.

When Carly answers the door, she seems surprised but happy to see us.

"I like your necklace," Carly says.

"I like your armband." I point to the black felt band on her arm.

"Nice job killing Ginger," Matt tells her.

I elbow him in the ribs and he shuts up.

Carly gets three of her mother's shovels and we dig holes on the side of the house near where she buried Ginger. We plant big clumps of daisies, then water them. It seems Carly's learned a lot about plants from her mom.

After we finish, we say a few words for Ginger.

"Ginger was a good hedgehog," Carly begins. "She gave everyone at our school so much pleasure. The Science Center won't be the same without her."

pleasure

Matt seems to have gotten over the fact that we're at Carly's house and adds some thoughts of his own. "Ginger stuck me with one of her quills last year, but I didn't mind. I hope they don't replace her with some lame animal like that gerbil we had in kindergarten who wouldn't even run on his stupid wheel."

"I hope that Ginger ends up in a prickle of great hedgehogs with lots of grapes and crickets," I say. Silently, I hope wherever Ginger ends up, she runs into Susan James and they can hang out for a while.

Mrs. Rodriquez brings us apple juice and chocolate chip cookies and tells us we did a great job with the plants.

"Hey, Matt," Carly says, "you want to steal a diamond?"

Matt seems confused, but for the first time today, Carly appears almost happy. We stay until dinnertime, dodging the motion detectors in Carly's basement, then designing a new system we'll set up next week—during our last few days of freedom.

See You Later,
Learning Camp

The final week of Learning Camp
reminds me of the last week of
school—neither the teachers nor
the students work too hard. Margot
lets us do our summer reading, even
helping us edit our reports. I spend
most days leaning against one of
the trees, slowly making my way
through the book Ms. Williams gave
me. It's hard, but I take my time. If

edit

Bodi could be here with me, I almost wouldn't mind.

Margot knows the book I'm reading, so at the end of every chapter I close my eyes and she asks me questions about what I see. Soon there are a bunch of us underneath the tree picturing the story in our heads. Afterward, I wonder how alike our scenes were, if we saw similar or different details. Then I come to my senses and join the water balloon fight in progress on the basketball court.

On the last day, Margot taps the side of her head when she says good-bye to me. "That imagination of yours can really help you. Make sure you use it."

I give her a wave, then race to my mother's car.

Since I've been back from the

Vineyard, I haven't seen Michael and Pedro because they were in San Diego on vacation. Today they're finally home, so we drive across town to see them.

When Michael answers the door, Pedro's on his lap in the wheelchair. Michael tells me about the basketball tournament in San Diego. They knew Pedro would be overwhelmed by the crowds, so they didn't take him to watch Michael play.

overwhelmed

I make a flip-o-rama out of my sketchbook and show Michael the story of my summer. I ask Michael if he can teach me more about how to animate my drawings on the computer.

We spend the rest of the afternoon making my pictures come to life onscreen. When we're done,

Michael burns them onto a DVD so I can show Dad.

But the most amazing part of the day isn't making my vocabulary words come to life, it's watching a different kind of movie. The facility where Pedro learned how to be a companion for humans made a video of Pedro in training. Michael shows me Pedro trying to turn on a light switch over and over again. Pedro makes several mistakes, but when he finally does it correctly, the trainer rings a bell to tell Pedro he succeeded at the task. I marvel at how Pedro doesn't get frustrated, just continues to try his best.

frustrated

In the next training exercise, a woman wearing scrubs aims a laser pointer at the "play" button on the DVD. Pedro fails at the task a million times, but when he finally gets it right, she gives him just as many compliments and hugs. It's embarrassing to admit, but Pedro takes direction better than I do.

"These tasks aren't natural activities for monkeys," Michael says. "It's amazing how they adapt."

adapt

I think about that first video and how much Pedro struggled with the light switch, then I look at him now, running to pick up the remote that Michael dropped. I cheer on the young Pedro in the video. *Don't give up. Believe it or not, you will master these tasks.*

I remember Ms. Williams talking about evolution in class last year. Maybe evolving is what we're supposed to do—all of us, all the time.

evolution

The Last Day
of Freedom

The next week and a half of summer flies by—I help Mom walk dogs at the "spa," learn new stunts with Matt, practice animation techniques with Dad, and build Carly's new burglar system. When I run into Joe Brennan at the playground, he tells me his new story about a duck that lays exploding eggs. It's not really a bad idea and I spend a few minutes collaborating with him. And I miss Grandma's chocolate cake with coconut frosting almost as much as I miss her, which is a lot.

Amy has left for college, so my parents let me accompany them on their Thursday-night date. At the Japanese restaurant, we take turns making up new inventions. I tell them I want to create a machine that slows down time so summer never ends.

"I assume you want one that speeds up time too," my father says, "so you can fast-forward through the school year."

"But then I'd miss the good stuff that happens—like hearing Bodi snore or getting a pet monkey." My mother shakes her head, but I get the feeling I'm wearing her down.

When the chef throws water on the fire, the flames rise three feet into the air. While everyone else oohs and aahs, I dive to the floor. "Fire!" I yell. "Stop, drop, and roll! Stop, drop, and roll."

Everyone laughs except Mom and Dad. Mom uses her chopsticks to point to my seat, and Dad slumps in his chair, but for a second I detect the beginning of a smile.

prevention

"Your son really took those fire prevention lessons to heart," another customer tells Mom.

"He's our pride and joy." She gives the man a huge smile while gripping my leg under the table like a vise.

I suddenly realize there are only a few days left until the first day of school and I haven't finished the book from Ms. Williams. But that doesn't stop me from bugging my parents to let us see a movie on the way home.

Or asking one more time about getting a monkey.

The Same Old Grind

My mother doesn't even try to buy new school clothes for me anymore. When the Day of Torture finally arrives, I wear my rattiest T-shirt as a form of protest. I haven't taken off the necklace from Lauren since she gave it to me, and I wonder if the gods will send down messages with answers to any pop quiz.

"Good-bye, Bodi, buddy." I stick

my face into his fur, hoping his comfy smell will get me through the day. I know I'll be counting the minutes till I see him waiting by the door for me after school.

A lot of the kids look different than they did a few months ago: Robert Orlando got glasses, Peter Chapman has braces, and Maria Ramsey grew at least three inches. Ms. Williams waves at me from her desk and smiles. I guess things could be worse than having a teacher who plays softball, loves dogs, and appreciates rock and roll.

After morning meeting—when can we stop having *those* things?—Ms. Williams asks us to read our book reports out loud. When she calls my name, I head to the front of the room.

"Derek, did you read three of the books on the list?"

"Uhm . . . one of them." I don't tell Ms. Williams my grandmother read a big chunk of it to me. "And I think I'm a more interesting character than any of the kids in those books."

determine

"That might be hard to determine, since you read only one of them."

"Good point."

"Can you tell us about the one you *did* read?"

"I can do more than that." I take my father's laptop from my pack and bring up the animation we worked on last week. The stick figures act out the book I read, the story of a boy and his dog.

When it's over, Ms. Williams wants to see it again, so we watch it one more time. She asks me questions about the characters, the setting, the plot, and I nail every one.

"Well," she finally says, "you didn't complete the assignment, but you definitely digested the book you did read. Between that and your animation, I guess we're even."

digested

A few months ago, Carly would've been furious that I didn't get into trouble, but now she smiles and gives me a thumbs-up. I can tell by Matt's face he wishes he had done some extra work too.

"I learned a few other things this summer," I continue. "That we all mess up sometimes and struggle with things that are difficult. That even if reading is hard, everyone needs stories. I didn't want to read the books on the list, but I wound up surrounded by stories anyway—a heroic dog, a brave monkey who learned to help an even braver boy, a girl who drowned, and the friend she left behind."

Ms. Williams leans back in her chair. "That's a lot of stories for one summer."

"That's what I'm saying—they're *everywhere*. I even met a woman who told herself a story about why her daughter died. It wasn't a true story, but it was an important one to help her deal with the pain."

I can tell some of the other kids are ready for me to sit down, but I keep going anyway.

"I also realized it's in our nature to learn new things. And that even though they're called permanent markers, they eventually do wear off. I also learned that avocados make messy cannonballs and monkeys can wear diapers."

"Okay, Derek. On to Maria."

"Also, if you spit into the wind on a ferry, it totally gets all over your face, and guys with muscles and Boston accents should *not* be tormented with poop."

tormented

"Thank you. It's Maria's turn now."

I slide into my seat, pretty proud of my report and animation project. I feel like a rock star until Maria takes out *her* laptop and presents a slide show she created to accompany all three books with music she wrote and performed on the cello in a dress she made during her summer sewing class.

cello

As my mother always asks, "Does it ever end?"

No, I don't think it does.

About the Author

author

Janet Tashjian is the author of many popular novels, including those in the Larry series—*The Gospel According to Larry*; *Vote for Larry*; *Larry and the Meaning of Life*—as well as *Fault Line*; *Multiple Choice*; and *Tru Confessions*. She lives with her family in Los Angeles, California.

About the Illustrator

illustrator

Jake Tashjian has been drawing pictures of his vocabulary words on index cards since he was in grade school (he's currently fifteen) and now has a stack taller than a house. Jake loves to walk his dog, Cinder, every morning.